"You've never slept with anybody till me, Trudy?"

Tru thought the self-satisfied grin tugging her lips was heart stopping, and when she lowered her head to his chest once more, he felt the curve of her smile on his bare skin. "Does heavy petting count?"

He shook his head. "No. Are you really telling me that before tonight, you'd never..."

"Now I have." With that Trudy traced a heart on his chest and drew an arrow through it.

He loved that she did that. She was amazing. She meshed with him on an intellectual level, and in bed she was insatiable. Now she was as cuddlesome as a kitten. "Why didn't you tell me?"

"Are you grilling me, Truman Steele?" she teased, squinting playfully as she fished around her ankles, pulling up a sheet to cover their naked bodies. "If so, I warn you I'm a force to be reckoned with."

"So I've discovered."

"Maybe you should call for backup," she quipped.

He kissed her lightly, affection that surprised him swelling his heart and spreading warmth through his limbs. "No backup," he warned. "I want you all to myself. I'm not sharing."

Dear Reader,

Ever since my miniseries BIG APPLE BABIES was released a few years ago by Harlequin American Romance, I've received letters from you, asking for another New York-set trilogy. And where better to introduce these sexy BIG APPLE BACHELORS than in Harlequin Temptation, where brothers Truman, Rex and Sullivan Steele can take a stand with Harlequin's hottest heroes?

The men you're about to meet are New York's finest. They hail from a great city with legendary heart that I love, and which I called home for many years. Because books are written long before publication, this fun-filled trilogy was completed before September 11, 2001, but I hope it pays tribute to those who serve and protect. Every other month this summer you'll meet a man from the NYPD, who I hope will deliver the Temptation promise: loving fantasies, pleasurable escape, sizzling sex and a happy ending!

With best wishes,

Jule McBride

**Meet all of New York's finest in the
BIG APPLE BACHELORS miniseries!**

Truman is *The Hotshot* in April 2002
Rex is *The Seducer* in June 2002
Sullivan is *The Protector* in August 2002

Jule McBride
The Hotshot

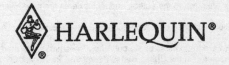

HARLEQUIN®

TORONTO • NEW YORK • LONDON
AMSTERDAM • PARIS • SYDNEY • HAMBURG
STOCKHOLM • ATHENS • TOKYO • MILAN • MADRID
PRAGUE • WARSAW • BUDAPEST • AUCKLAND

To all those who serve and protect,
especially those in Manhattan on September 11

ISBN 0-373-25975-1

THE HOTSHOT

Copyright © 2002 by Julianne Moore.

Visit us at www.eHarlequin.com

Printed in U.S.A.

1

"MA WON THE LOTTERY?" Truman Steele was still unable to believe it. The jackpot had been growing for weeks, and because it was June first and another hot, steamy New York summer was right around the corner, people had been amusing themselves by speculating about the lucky winner on subways, street corners, and around office watercoolers. Every day, the TV news depicted long lines outside delis and street kiosks where people waited to buy tickets, and the *New York News* had been running man-in-the-street interviews, asking people what they'd do if they won the huge windfall.

Truman had told himself he'd buy a fishing boat, maybe vacation in Vegas and invest in blue-chip stocks, but now that he might actually get a third of the money, he wasn't so sure. He needed to rethink his game plan. Wearing the NYPD's standard-issue navy uniform, he stretched his long legs, then put one hand on his holster and paced to and fro in his oldest sibling's childhood bedroom. Sullivan's room was where the three brothers had retreated to mull over family crises since time immemorial.

Not that winning fifteen million dollars was a crisis, exactly. *At least not yet,* thought Truman, releasing a throaty whistle. "I must have bought thirty tickets."

"Me, too," confessed Rex, who'd kicked off dirty

sneakers so he could lie on a neatly made twin bed so small it was hard to imagine Sullivan Steele ever occupying it. The only brother to work undercover, Rex was a master of disguises. He'd come from a stakeout looking homeless, sporting a scraggly black beard, baggy, oil-stained jeans and a questionably perfumed trench coat, which he'd thankfully left outside.

"You buy any tickets, Sully?" asked Rex.

Sullivan shook his head. "Waste of money," said the oldest, thrusting his hands into the pockets of gray suit trousers. "At least I thought so."

"What were you going to do if you won, Rex?" asked Truman.

Vanish and start a whole new life, thought Rex, picturing himself wearing white, rolled-up trousers while combing a beach for shells. His throat constricted as he glanced away. Unlike his brothers, Rex had never wanted to be a cop, although he rarely admitted it, even to himself. Rex was still haunted by how scared he'd been as a kid every morning when their father holstered his gun and left for work. He'd always waited for the evening Augustus Steele wouldn't make it home for dinner, and because Rex wouldn't put another kid through that worry, he'd long ago decided that having a family and working for the NYPD didn't mix. He finally shrugged. "I don't know. Fifteen million's a lot of dough, little brother."

"Sure is," agreed Truman, staring through a window into the courtyard, admiring a leafy jungle of trees, bushes and ferns. Before Sheila Steele had been blessed with one of the biggest lottery wins in New York history, she'd also been the more modest recipient of a green thumb and a brownstone. Situated on

Bank Street in the West Village, the Steeles' home had been handed down through Sheila's family, and because of the expense of maintaining it in Manhattan, the upper two floors were rented to tenants. From the front, despite cheerful green shutters, the place remained somewhat gloomy, a massive stone edifice on a gray street, banked by gray sidewalks and equally gray parking meters. Tourists would never guess at the bright, cozy interior, or the sprawling riot of plants and flowers Sheila kept thriving in the courtyard in back.

"Fifteen *million*," Truman said again. "Five each."

Sully shook his head, the same wary suspicion in his eyes that had made him, at thirty-six, the youngest cop in New York to become captain of a precinct. "If Ma hadn't shown us the letter from the lottery board, I wouldn't have believed her."

Rex chuckled. "Don't be so suspicious, Sully. This is Ma we're talking about. Not a criminal."

"Beg to differ," countered Truman. "Correct me if I'm wrong, but didn't Ma just say she expects us to find *wives?* And if we don't, she's going to give all that money away to a foundation that saves *sea turtles?*"

"They also save marine iguanas," reminded Rex.

"And don't forget the flightless cormorants," added Sullivan dryly.

"Oh, right," whispered Truman. "Flightless cormorants."

At that, the three brothers simply stared at each other in shock. Rex's shoulders started shaking with suppressed laughter, then Sullivan gave in, cracking a grin, and then Truman said, "What the *hell* is a flightless cormorant, anyway?"

"A bird, I think," said Sully.

But that wasn't confirmed, since suddenly, none of the men had the breath to talk. Sully gasped, clapping Rex's shoulder affectionately, and Truman doubled, slapping his knee and laughing until he was wiping tears from his eyes. Each was contemplating the life-altering, past half hour of their lives.

When their mother invited them home for lunch, they'd thought nothing of it, of course. Sullivan and Truman rented apartments nearby and ate here regularly, and although Rex lived in Brooklyn, he often dropped by. No, the invitation was nothing special, but *after* lunch, Sheila had shown them a receipt from the lottery board whom, she said, would be contacting them. She'd put the money she'd won into a special account already, but since Sullivan, Rex and Truman would be the probable beneficiaries, the board needed them to sign some papers. "The money's yours, boys," Sheila had finished brightly.

Truman was still watching her in stunned silence, when she'd added, "But only if you marry within the next three months."

She'd kept flashing that brilliant smile as if she'd said the most reasonable thing in the world, and Truman had shaken his head. He loved his mother, they all did, but she was the world's most unlikely woman to birth three cops, or to have married one. Every inch the Earth Mother, she stayed too busy to do more than twist her long gray hair into a haphazard bun, and she favored ankle-length skirts, vests and sandals that she wore with socks. Unconventional to say the least, she had a ready smile and heart of gold that allowed her to not only mother her own sons, but often the men in the precincts for which they worked. Her special homemade doughnuts, complete with blue-and-gold icing, were legendary.

"Ma can be a little nuts sometimes," admitted Rex when his chuckles subsided. "But it's a good kind of nuts."

Truman had his doubts. During lunch, the first thing he'd said was, "Where did you get an idea like this, Ma?"

"Oh, I read about such things all the time," she'd assured, nodding toward a novel she'd left open on a chaise longue.

"In *books*," Truman had stressed. "*Novels.*" Half-afraid his mother hadn't understood, he'd added, "Books are *make-believe.*"

"Not anymore, son." Laughing, Sheila had wagged a finger in warning. "No fake marriages, either, boys. And you have to be in love. You can't cheat and get married, planning to divorce later. Nor can you tell your prospective brides that marrying them will make you rich."

"That takes away a bargaining chip," muttered Truman, who had absolutely no intention of getting married. At least not for love. For money, sure. But he'd nearly married for love once—and never again.

Frowning, Sheila had added, "And unless all three of you find brides and marry within the three months, nobody gets any money at all."

"We all *three* have to get married," clarified Truman.

She'd nodded. "Yes. And in order to make sure your future wives don't know about the money, we'll have to keep this hush-hush. If anyone, including the newspapers, finds out I won, I'm going to donate the money to the Research Foundation of the Galapagos Islands."

"The Galapagos Islands?" Sully had repeated in disbelief.

Their father, like Sully, was rational to a fault. He'd put an end to the ridiculous plan. "Where's Dad?" Truman had demanded.

For a moment, their mother had looked distant. "Work," she'd murmured. "He's been putting in a lot of overtime. I think a big case is breaking, and I've been meaning to talk to you three about it. I'm not sure, but I think your father might be in some sort of trouble—"

"Have you talked to him about this?" Rex had interrupted, since this was hardly the first time Augustus Steele had been in trouble or working too hard. The man was always putting out fires downtown in the commissioner's office at Police Plaza.

"No," Sheila had returned. "I haven't talked to him, and now that you mention it, I'd better make another stipulation. If you tell your father about this, the deal's off, and every dime goes to the Galapagos Islands."

Sully's expression was usually unreadable, but his lips had parted in frank astonishment. "You're not telling Pop you won the lottery?"

"Nope," Sheila had returned, twisting a leather wristband to get a better look at a watch that had more gadgets on it than the dashboard of a Ferrari. "And neither are you. Now, boys, I've got a few more minutes before my meeting with C.L.A.S.P."

Truman had gaped at her. How could she run off at a time such as this? "C.L.A.S.P.?"

"City and Local Activists for Street People," she'd clarified, her lips pursing in displeasure. "The mayor cut funding again. Three more mental health facilities closed this morning, and hundreds of people have been released with nowhere to go. We're opening a new women's shelter in the meat-packing district. This week, I'll post flyers in your precincts, asking for clothing donations. I've been putting them all over town for months. Everybody needs to contribute."

She'd paused, shaking her head in disgust. "Even Ed Koch and David Dinkins were better than *this*," she'd said, her tone maligning the previous New York mayors. "Anyway, before I leave, why don't you go to Sullivan's room and think over my proposition? Let me know if you want to—" Pushing aside her pique over New York City politics, she'd grinned, enjoying the catbird seat. "Accept my challenge."

She hadn't looked the least bit fazed by her remarkable win, and Truman guessed it was largely because she was the mother of three cops. Nothing ruffled her. "I'll be anxious to see who makes it to the finish line first. You boys with your brides, or my poor tortoises in the Galapagos."

"Tortoises," Truman whispered now.

"What else?" murmured Sullivan.

Preserving natural animal habitats in the Galapagos Islands had long been their mother's obsession, so the brothers had been weaned on stories about the mysterious volcanic islands in the Pacific. Just off the coast of Ecuador, the islands were close to a mainland that was magical in its own right, with a history of Inca warriors, Amazon explorers and Spanish conquistadors. Nature had been left to thrive on its own in that lost part of the world, and the islands that had inspired Charles Darwin's theory of evolution in the 1830s were now home to wildlife that existed nowhere else on earth.

"Don't get me wrong," Truman said to his brothers now, feeling a twinge of guilt. "I've got nothing against sea turtles."

Sully chuckled. "Me, neither." He let a beat pass, then added with irony, "It's the marine iguanas that get on *my* nerves."

"Oh, I don't know," joked Rex. "Penguins can be such a pain." He sighed, adding, "What's happening in the islands is pretty nasty. Ma's right. They're still trying to clean up the last oil spill. A couple days ago, some ship, I think it was called the—"

"*Eliza*," supplied Sullivan.

"The *Eliza*," repeated Rex. "Right. It ran aground near a nesting area for sea lion pups."

"Ma's serious," Truman reminded. "Are we doing this or not?"

Rex stared. "We can't find soul mates in three months."

"She said wives, not soul mates," argued Truman.

"To me, a wife *would be* a soul mate," returned Rex.

"Oh, please," muttered Truman. As the only Steele who'd ever given true love a whirl, he knew better.

"Ma said we have to be in love," Sully put in.

"For five million dollars," Truman said, calculating a third of the pie, "I think I could lie."

Sully tried to look shocked. "To your own *mother?*"

"As if I don't have enough on my plate..." Truman raked a hand through light brown hair, the longest strands of which traced a strong jaw.

Rex raised an eyebrow. "Why? What happened?"

"Coombs is trying to put me on a two-week drive-along with a reporter from the *New York News*."

Coombs was Truman's boss at Manhattan South precinct.

"Smart move. You're the best-looking cop in the NYPD," said Sully without rancor. "You've got a strong arrest record, and you're chasing the limelight, little brother."

Truman tamped down his anger. It was tourist season, which meant the mayor, the *News,* and the NYPD were seeking ways to curb the mob hysteria that inevitably came with summer heat waves, and to assure people that New York City was the perfect place to bring kids on vacation.

Truman wasn't interested in the public relations article. He was determined to solve the city's latest, high-profile case, which had been dubbed the Glass Slipper case by the *New York News.* The case had been assigned to him, but if he wound up doing a drive-along with a reporter, he wouldn't have time to work it. He had too many other more important cases on his desk. The Glass Slipper was special, though, since it involved film celebrities and rock stars. Cracking it would garner Truman enough attention to get him his full detective's shield. He loved his work, hated bogus cases, and was tired of moving up the rung so much more slowly than his brothers.

"And now I'm supposed to find a *wife?*" he muttered.

"Speaking of women and your patrol car," said Rex, fishing in his pocket for a piece of paper. "Some girl left this under your windshield wiper. I brought it in. Maybe you can marry her."

Truman glanced down at a note written in lipstick.

*Officer Steele, I saw your car. Nice meeting you yesterday.
I'd really like to get together for dinner. Call me. Candy.*

Truman had enjoyed meeting her, too. Unfortunately, he'd been arresting her for being drunk and disorderly. Carefully pocketing the note in case his search
for a bride came to that, he leaned in the doorway,
glancing away from Sully's room and the model planes
and boats Sully had spent hours building as a kid, into
Rex's room, which was full of books, and then to his
own, which was decorated with sports trophies and
school pennants.

"Candy's cute, huh?" asked Rex, referring to the
note.

"Drunk and disorderly," corrected Truman.

"But there will be others," Sully said dryly, making
Truman smile. Truman never beat his older brothers at
anything, but Sully was right. Truman attracted the
most women. He enjoyed their company, too. He just
didn't want to set up housekeeping. Until now. How
would his mother know whether or not he really loved
his bride? She wouldn't, he decided, a new goal forming in his mind. In addition to cracking the Glass Slipper case, he'd be the first Steele to marry—though not
for love, of course.

"As soon as my latest case broke," Rex was saying,
"I was going to take vacation. I've racked up four
weeks leave time."

Sully raised his eyebrows. "Where?"

Rex offered a typical Rex response. "Wherever the
wind takes me."

"It better be some place with women," Truman
warned. "Seeing as we've only got three months to get
married."

Three months. Or they'd lose fifteen million dollars. "Can you guys believe this?" Sully said rhetorically. The way he saw it, they might as well hand the money over to the turtles right now. His last serious, long-term relationship had lacked passion he couldn't live without, and when he'd found passion, the relationship hadn't included a meeting of the minds.

Absently, Sully reached for a shelf, lifting one of the models he'd made as a kid—a ship inside a bottle. Rarely given to whimsical behavior—that was Rex's domain—Sully imagined himself writing a letter detailing what he wanted in a bride, putting it in the bottle and tossing it into the Hudson River. All his life, he'd done the tried and true...the dinner dates, boxes of candy, bouquets of flowers, and he was still single. For years, he'd wanted the kind of relationship his parents shared. Why not send a message in a bottle...?

"It's us or the turtles," Truman prompted.

"Well, Truman," returned Sully, thoughtfully turning the bottle in his hands and surveying the ship inside, a classic Spanish galleon of a sort that had comprised treasure fleets and been manned by sixteenth century pirates. "Maybe the reporter from the *News* will be female, and you can marry *her.*"

"Right." Truman smirked. "The *News* always sends a guy on the drive-alongs."

"YOU'RE SENDING ME ON A drive-along? With the *NYPD*? For two full weeks?" Trudy Busey didn't try to hide her disappointment. She told herself she was a trained professional and needed to prove she could be cool under fire, but as she glanced around the table and took in her co-workers, among them Scott Smith-

Sanker who, as usual, was getting all the juicy assignments, she decided there was only one way to claim turf in a newsroom—fight.

The city editor, Dimitri Slovinsky, otherwise known as Dimi, raised a bushy eyebrow. Overweight, over fifty and slovenly in appearance, only the sharp bite in his dark eyes gave away his superior intelligence. "Are you having a problem, Busey?"

She braced herself, wishing Dimi would trust her with bigger stories. Scott wanted her to quit the *News*. And her own father, who owned the *Milton Herald* in West Virginia never took her dreams seriously. Yesterday, Terrence Busey had the nerve to call the *News* a "mere tabloid."

This, she thought now, from the man who, before semiretirement, had handed the *Milton Herald* over to her brothers, Bob and Ed. The weekly's circulation had dropped by 50 subscribers, and now only went to 300 households. None of which would be happening if her father had named her his successor. His lack of belief in her hurt, cutting to the core. Why couldn't he see she was a good reporter? Why couldn't Dimi?

Despite her loyalty to the *Milton Herald,* Trudy loved everything about this paper that had started in 1803 as the *New York Evening News* and faithfully served New York ever since, becoming the longest continuously running daily newspaper in America. She loved how the smell of ink filled her nostrils as she pushed through the smudged glass doors every morning carrying coffee from Starbucks. She loved being greeted by the sight of harried reporters who'd been awake all night at desks strewn with overflowing ashtrays, foam cups and files.

Without even looking, Trudy could name the blow-ups of past *News* covers hanging on the walls: the Kennedy Assassination, the Lindbergh baby, the Wall Street Crash of 1929, the murder of mob kingpin, Paul Castellano...

The *News* was a hub. Its reporters had earned nearly forty Pulitzer prizes, and every time she walked through its doors, Trudy realized her finger was on the pulse of America. She had no interest in the conservative *New York Times*. She'd been raised on a hometown paper, and the *News* had hometown roots—in the country's biggest hometown.

"Dimi," she began, fighting frustration, but determined to defend her position. "There are so many great stories begging to be written. The drive-along isn't the best use of my time."

It was an understatement. The drive-along was pure fluff. Human interest. Good publicity the *News* generated every year as a favor to the mayor at the beginning of tourist season.

Dimi eyed her. "What did you have in mind?"

"The Glass Slipper story."

"Scott's on that."

Of course he is. She tried not to react, but the mere mention of Scott Smith-Sanker's name sent her through the roof. If he scooped her once more on a story that was rightfully hers, she was going to implode. "Well, what about the lottery?" she suggested. "Whoever claimed the fifteen-million-dollar jackpot wants to remain anonymous. We need to find out who it was. After all our hype, the public wants to know." The story was every bit as important as the Glass Slipper.

"Ben's following up on the lottery."

It wasn't easy to tamp down her anger. "There was a murder just twenty minutes ago on the East Side. What about that?"

"Keith's headed there already."

"Okay," she said patiently. "It's not a city story, but we need to follow up on the *Eliza*." She glanced toward a *News* cover showing the oil tanker that had run aground near the Galapagos Islands.

"A stringer's on it."

Not about to worsen the situation by making a scene, Trudy waited until the meeting was over and the others filed out before turning to her boss and saying exactly what was on her mind. "If this is the kind of work you want me to do, why did you even bother to hire me?"

"Your assignment's a good one, Trudy."

"It's busy work," she pushed back.

"High profile. You'll liaise with the mayor."

Maybe. But that wasn't the kind of reporter she was meant to be. She'd had this same conversation with her father and brother for years, whenever they handed her grunt work, hoping to discourage her from working for the *Herald*. The ploy had worked. She'd left the *Herald* in a huff. But she was *not* leaving the *New York News*, and she intended to get real stories. The hard stuff.

"The *Glass Slipper*," she reminded, not usually one to toot her own horn, but understanding she no longer had a choice. "I thought of calling it that. The name sold papers, Dimi. The allusion to Cinderella and Prince Charming captured the imagination of our readership."

The case had begun two months ago when wealthy,

famous female New Yorkers began reporting the bizarre theft of expensive, custom-made shoes. At this point, over a hundred pairs were missing from over a hundred apartments, and the police, unable to discern a motive and confused by how the thief gained access to so many well-guarded homes, were hot to solve the crimes.

Trudy had written the *News*'s first headline, "Can These Cinderellas Find Their Glass Slippers?" Her next was, "Who is Prince Charming?" Ever since, along with the growing lottery jackpot, the story had captured the imagination of news-hungry New Yorkers. Newspaper sales had skyrocketed.

"Circulation's up," she continued. "And **we're** getting more hits online, too."

"Your contribution's been noticed," Dimi conceded. "And soon, Trudy, we'll have a hot tip that's—"

"Right for me?" She wasn't in the habit of cutting off her boss, but she'd reached the end of her rope. "I've been here two years. I've been patient. I've gophered. I've gotten coffee, picked up lunch and worked double time. Just how many dues do you expect me to pay before you'll let me wedge a toe in your old buddy club?"

Dimi considered. "You think this is a chauvinist atmosphere?"

"How could I *not* feel discriminated against?" she returned, not backing down. She'd have left before now, but she wanted the experience of working on the nation's longest running daily, even if she cursed the ambition that made her want to conquer it. She could almost hear her father's voice. "You're cute, Trudy. If you want to go into news, why don't you try television?" Occasionally, he'd generously point to weather girls as models.

Trudy Busey was no weather girl.

Dimi stared at her as he peeled silver foil from a roll of antacids and began chewing one—all the while thinking he ought to give in and do what doctors kept telling him: lose weight. But then, doctors didn't understand the pressures of being an editor in a big-city newsroom, no more than the stress of managing people like Trudy. She wanted the Glass Slipper and lottery stories? Well, the distressing fact was, she deserved them.

"Why did you bother to hire me?" she asked again.

Because she'd possessed two main prerequisites for the job, Dimi thought now. She was eager and pushy. During their interview, she'd been fiercely determined. Along with college newspaper clippings, she'd submitted human interest stories she'd written for her father's newspaper, and Dimi easily read between the lines. Her father didn't want her in the news business, but she was hell-bent on succeeding, not to mention jealous of two, less talented brothers who'd been handed the *Milton Herald* on a platter.

Dimi had wanted to give her a chance. Trouble was, one look at Trudy, and Dimi wished he was thirty years younger, fifty pounds lighter, and a much nicer guy. She was the one person in years who'd actually located his soft spot. Once he'd given her the job, he simply couldn't stand to set her loose in a town he feared would eat her alive.

She was petite. Five foot four, with smooth skin and fine, yellow-blond hair that just touched her shoulders. Every time he looked at her, Dimi understood her father's sentiments. There was something pure and un-touched about her, evidenced by how Scott Smith-Sanker slid stories out from under her with the ease of a well-lubricated machine. Dimi feared, once she was on the street, her soft West Virginia twang would peg her as an easy mark, too. How could he train her wide, adventuresome eyes on a crime scene? Or put her in a position to get chewed up by angry cops and hustlers? Leave that to the Scott Smith-Sankers of the world, Dimi thought now. Guys like Scott were born and bred for life's ugliness.

Trudy had been watching him, trying to guess what was going on inside his mind, and now she told herself not to say it, but then did. "Please," she said, hating begging. "At least give me the lottery story. Or the Ga-lapagos oil spill."

Looking guilty, he shook his head. "You're on the drive-along with a cop from Manhattan South named Truman Steele. And you better get moving."

She was stuck with a poster boy for the NYPD, Trudy thought angrily as Dimi gave her the rundown. Truman Steele was from a family of cops, with a father in the Commissioner's office in Police Plaza and two brothers in downtown precincts. Her mind still on the Galapagos Islands, the lottery and the Glass Slipper story, she glazed, regaining her attention when Dimi said, "Manhattan South is—"

"I know where the precinct is," she snapped, her voice steely as Dimi thrust a file into her hand.

Right before tucking it under her arm, she glimpsed a photo of the most interesting-looking man she'd ever seen. Her heart clutched. Truman Steele was bare-chested and seated in the open door of a patrol car.

Sucking in a breath, she realized this was one of the candied photos the NYPD's public relations department had posted around the city last year, depicting cops out of uniform, so they'd seem more accessible to the public.

Her eyes skated over a smooth, muscled chest, unable to ignore that the nipples were erect, as if the picture had been taken on a cold day. The face was unusual in a way she'd rather not notice. Very arresting. Flyaway wisps of straight, light brown hair fell longer than the police force usually allowed, with the longest strands tracing a hard, implacable jaw. His skin was taut, molded over noticeably rigid bones, and he had a wide mouth and nose, which, along with dark, cautious eyes that tilted upward, made him appear to have Asian blood, though he was clearly caucasian.

That strange mix of features came together in a one-of-a-kind face that would have been eye-catching enough without the quality of the expression. Instead of looking as if he was posing for a photo, Truman looked as if he were staring across a candlelit table, his lips parting to ask a woman if she wanted to make love. Even worse, given the composition of the picture, it was only natural that Trudy's gaze follow the downward arc of an arm, to where a wrist rested on a jeans clad hip. Loosely curled fingers unintentionally covered the V at his open legs. Belatedly realizing her eyes were fixed on that spot, she quickly glanced away, not about to acknowledge the disappointment she'd felt when she hadn't...seen more.

"I remember when the NYPD took these press kits photos of the cops," she managed, telling herself she wasn't affected.

"Do you?" Dimi said, looking mildly amused.

"Yes," she said succinctly. "I do."

Still smiling, Dimi added, "Don't forget you're on the job, Busey."

"I won't," she assured simply. As a rule, Trudy kept men at arm's length. Between fighting her father and brothers, not to mention Dimi and Scott Smith-Sanker, she found it hard enough to realize her ambitions.

The last thing she needed was another man dragging her down.

2

"I'M WORKING WITH *HER?*" Truman glanced from Coombs's glassed-in office, across an open squad room, to his own office where Trudy Busey was seated on a gray metal foldout chair. Her back was turned away from the glass and the squad room's chaos—a jumble of ringing telephones, noisy computer printers, outraged victims giving statements and perpetrators protesting arrest.

Coombs, a hardened fifty-year-old cop, was staring at Truman through ice-green eyes. Coombs had a few wisps of hair left, a gym-honed physique and was wearing an off-the-rack navy suit so like the NYPD's standard-issue uniform that Truman wondered why he bothered wearing civvies at all. "Ms. Busey seems nice," Coombs said. "What's your problem?"

"What's *my* problem?" Truman took in Trudy's back. Fine strands of straight blond hair, more yellow than gold, hung to her shoulders. She wore a blue-gray blazer, and without looking, he could imagine a matching skirt and pumps. He was usually happy to meet the Trudy Busey type—but not today.

"Who is she?" he asked rhetorically. "Some ivy league intern who got a summer job at the *News?*" He raised a staying hand. "No, don't tell me. She goes to Vassar. She's not even getting paid for this, and her father got her the job?"

Coombs considered. "What makes you say that?"

As if greater-than-average detection skills were needed. "Given the way she's dressed, she thinks she's going to a tea party, not on a drive-along."

"As I've explained, you're off your usual patrol route, so for all practical purposes Ms. Busey *is* going to a tea party. While she's with you, I want this city to look as clean as a bathtub. No," he corrected, "for Ms. Busey, make it a champagne fountain."

"What about the Glass Slipper case?"

"Reassigned. Capote and Dern are on it."

Truman stared in mute protest. The two cops couldn't burn their way out of candle wax. "They won't solve it."

"No, but I'd rather let them bungle a celebrity shoe theft than an Upper East Side murder, and that was my choice this morning." Sighing, Coombs added, "Don't quote me on that. I'm on your side, Steele, but these PR gigs are important."

The information went down hard. "You know, Chief," Truman finally said, his tone understated, "I'm not real happy about this."

"Rome wasn't built in a day, but you've got two weeks with this woman," returned Coombs. "That means whatever work I don't reassign to Capote and Dern, you'll be handling in your spare time. Now, be nice to Ms. Busey. She looks like a sweetheart. And you need a haircut," added Coombs. "Sorry, but it's regulation."

"Be nice," Truman muttered, heading for his desk, eyes locked on Trudy. Since the story was pure public relations, Truman had hoped the *News* would send a cynical, seasoned Dan Rather type. They'd shoot some pool or sit in the cruiser, drinking espressos while jointly working up material for the article. Truman had figured this would take the better part of an afternoon, then he'd be back on his beat.

And now this. Breezing into his office, he circled the gray metal desk, seated himself, pushed aside a foot-high stack of manila files stained by brown coffee cup rings, then repositioned the computer monitor. When he was comfortable, he slowly lifted his gaze—only to find himself staring into eyes so astonishing he was glad he was sitting down.

His chest got too tight as those eyes captured his, and their quality—bright, alert and intelligent—so held his attention that, at first, Truman didn't even realize they were blue. When he did, he was jolted back to his senses. He felt as if he'd left his body, only to have his sensations return with a trace of her in each of them. Sight came with a vision of blue eyes, scent with a breath of floral perfume, hearing with her soft catch of breath, and touch with the urge to reach across the desk for her.

Taste, unfortunately, was left to Truman's active imagination. She was clean-cut, fresh-faced, and nearly everything about her made him think of white bras, barely there makeup and Dentyne ads. Except for those eyes. They were sharp and oddly, irresistibly invasive, full of such frank curiosity that he was immediately sure she'd be great in bed.

Her mouth wasn't nearly as interesting as her eyes, but it was pleasant enough, the lips wider and fuller than her face called for and, unfortunately, thinning into a tight smile.

"You're Mr. Steele then?"

"Then," he assured. "As well as before and after."

"And I thought I was the wordsmith."

They were definitely getting off to a good start. He now saw that her yellow-blond hair was slightly layered in front, framing a gently curving jaw. What could a woman this pretty be so angry about? "You must be the reporter."

She nodded curtly. "Good. I'm in the right place."

He wished he didn't feel so strangely electrified, as if she'd just shot something scalding into his bloodstream. "Looks like it."

Tugging a file from under her arm, she opened it on his desk, displaying his picture. "Nice to meet you, too," she said dryly, and then, as if reading his mind, "I hope you don't mind me asking, but what are *you* so mad about?" She tapped a finger to his picture. "Bad hair day, Mr. Steele?"

He should have known the NYPD PR department would courier that file over to the *News*. In the candid photo, he was bare-chested, wearing hip-hugging jeans and seated in an open-doored squad car, looking for all the world like a *Playgirl* model. Bad hair day, indeed. "The LAPD was getting a lot of bad publicity, and our PR department was afraid there'd be some spillover," he found himself defending.

At the bottom of the photo were interview bullet-points that Trudy Busey now began reading in a voice that twanged like a softly played banjo. "Truman Steele," she began. "Height, six feet. Weight—one-eighty. Residence—Greenwich Village. Hobbies—Scuba Diving, Raquetball, Skiing..."

When she was done, he said, "And you're Trudy

Busey. Given the twang in your voice, I take it you're not from around here?"

"What did you do to reach that startling conclusion? Sift through mountains of forensic evidence?"

Oh, yes. They were definitely getting off to a stellar start. But she hadn't known him long enough to hate him. "In case they didn't teach you this at Vassar, we cops don't always have a say in what goes on. And that includes whether or not we get our pictures taken."

"Looks to me like you enjoyed posing."

He'd tried to make the best out of it. "You say that as if you think ideas might be beyond my limited capacity."

"Are they?"

"You've got two weeks to find out." Vague disappointment coiled inside him, and he realized he was hoping to coax a genuine smile from her. But she wasn't the type to crack. He leaned over the messy desk, his eyes finding hers. His smile hovered between mild bemusement and annoyance. Holding up a file, he said, "Do you know what this is, Ms. Busey?"

Her eyes slightly widened. "Is this a test?" Trudy squinted harder, then guessed, "A file folder?"

He smirked. "Cute." But she *was* dangerously cute. "It *looks* like a file. But really, it's one of the twenty unsolved murders on my desk. Murders that won't get solved because of this bogus assignment. This is Manhattan. We get four a day."

He barely noticed she'd flipped open a notebook and started jotting. "So, you say you usually cover about twenty cases?"

Sighing, he realized she was probably a dynamite reporter. "Yeah," he said, none too happy that the assignment with her meant working those cases in his spare time.

"With or without a partner?"

"Usually with. Mine just quit."

Her lips twitched. "Let me guess. You didn't get along with him?"

"She was transferred to Police Plaza."

Trudy was surprised. "Your partner was a woman?"

His ability to work with the opposite sex was probably why he'd gotten stuck with Trudy, not that he'd mention it. "She still is. And we got along. Usually my encounters with women aren't nearly this antagonistic."

She almost smiled. "Maybe I've got more important things to do today, too, Officer Steele. Did you ever think of that?"

So that was it. She'd guessed he'd been complaining to Coombs. And no, Truman had assumed she'd be thrilled to ride around with a cop. Most women liked it. "Important things?" he couldn't help but say. "Lunch at the Plaza? Or maybe a hot story's breaking at the museum? Ah—" he nodded sympathetically "—new baby pandas at the zoo?"

He hadn't riled her. "The pandas are in San Diego. This week our mayor's made budget cuts, and I thought I'd be at the closing of a psychiatric hospital this morning. That's why I'm dressed this way. For the record, I didn't ask to be here."

Guess she'd told him. "Well, since you're here, I'm glad you wore that suit because we'll be zipping around the fancy-schmancy Upper East Side these next two weeks, fining well-heeled women with poodles who forget to scoop up the doggy-do." He smiled. "If things get really hectic, maybe you'll even see me haul in a jaywalker."

Trudy shot him a steady look. "I'm hoping for that special someone who didn't put the extra quarter in the meter."

"Only if I'm not too busy ticketing unleashed dogs."

"Look," Trudy said, all pretense vanishing. "Don't blame me. If your PR people quit coming up with these assignments—"

He stared incredulously. "The *News* is the problem. Your boss is racking up favors from the mayor again by making the city look like Kansas."

"Kansas can get nasty. Look what happened to Dorothy."

He sighed. "How long have you been working there, anyway?"

"Long enough."

"Ah. You're bright and ambitious, but the boys aren't letting you get ahead?"

He'd struck a nerve. "Two years," she muttered.

Suddenly, he felt sorry for her. Already, he could tell she was smarter than most reporters he'd met. Realizing he was staring at her like a besotted fool, he averted his gaze, and the file he'd been holding slipped between his fingers. Cursing, he quickly tried to grab the grisly color photos that fanned over his desk. They were from a shooting death in a crack house near Penn Station. "Sorry," he murmured.

Her voice was cool, her pen poised. "Why don't you guys get file cabinets? Budget problems? Any comment?"

There were budget problems, of course, and yes, he'd like to comment, but she was unnerving him.

First, it was clear she meant to turn her public-relations story into something more in-depth, which would infuriate their bosses. And the grisly photos hadn't even phased her. "How'd a girl like you wind up with such a poker face?"

"I'm not a child."

Curiouser and curiouser, he thought. Trudy Busey apparently moved through the world expecting to be patronized. His cop's instincts got the best of him. "Who treats you like a kid?"

"I'm not the interview subject. You are."

Subject. He wasn't used to hearing himself reduced to that. "Well, now you know how it feels."

"Sorry, but like I said, I didn't ask to be here."

No, and it was starting to annoy him. "Most people like cops. We're the good guys. The heroes."

She chuckled. "Unless you're on the take."

"You don't quit, do you?"

"Tenacity," she returned. "A good trait in reporters."

He went for her weak spot. "Maybe not so good in a woman."

She rose swiftly. She was slender and economical, without a shiver of wasted movement. With a full-frontal view, he could see that her conservative outfit left hints of temptation: an extra button undone at the throat, a lace bra visible through the blouse, a skirt just tight enough to mold the sexy rounding of her tummy. He'd bet every penny of his coming five million that the legs he couldn't see were shapely enough to model panty hose, and that she treated them to top-drawer silk stockings.

Just as her fisted hands landed knuckle-down on the

desk, he caught a glimpse of a diamond. His heart plunged, then he registered the diamond was on the right hand, not the left. He was a cop, so usually he got details like that straight. Not that he'd noticed wedding rings before his mother's recent challenge. "C'mon," he murmured, realizing he'd risen with her and now reseated himself. "Why don't you sit back down?"

"Because you're attacking me. And because I'd rather be working on the mental hospitals, the lottery, or the Galapagos oil spill."

Hardly wanting to contemplate the Galapagos Islands and the lottery, he gave Trudy another once-over. She was tougher than she looked, and he liked her dedication. Still, those eyes were made to soften. Already, he knew how the blue irises would temper to gray, how the sharp edges of the gaze would blur until her eyes turned as vaporous as smoke.

"Why are you staring at me?" she asked, point-blank.

Because he was crossing her off his list of potential brides. Trudy Busey was far too interesting, and he was looking for a woman who'd marry him, knowing she'd soon be divorced. Mulling over the five million dollars coming to him, he calculated the sum, minus what he'd pay in alimony. "Because I'm thinking about how to proceed," he said. "You're going to make me, this precinct and the streets of New York look great, right?"

"You say that as if I'm a sellout," she said indignantly. "As if a reporter's not really needed to write this story."

He gentled his voice. "There's some truth to that."

"Let's get one thing straight," she shot back. "This assignment is my idea of hell."

Before he could respond, he saw his mother enter the squad room, carrying a stack of flyers, probably asking for clothing donations for the homeless. As much as Truman loved the woman, she had a knack for showing up at the worst moments. He could almost hear her saying, "Ah, so you've found your bride!"

Which meant he had about three minutes to get rid of Trudy. Maybe five, seeing as his mother had stopped to talk to Capote and Dern, who'd been salivating around the watercooler ever since they'd been handed the Glass Slipper case, however temporarily.

"Before we go," he said, "I've got a few things to take care of here." Closing the file with his picture in it, he pushed it across the desk, toward Trudy. "My cruiser's in the garage downstairs."

"The one with the dice hanging over the rearview mirror?"

"Cute," he said again. "Mind waiting? I'll meet you there. Twenty minutes."

"No problem." She offered a curt nod. Sweeping the file off his desk, she turned, hugging it to her chest, and he whistled softly, watching her weave through the squad room. He'd been right about the legs. Long and shapely, they were encased in shimmering summer hose. The gentle twitch of her backside could make dry cotton salivate.

He didn't really have any work to do. He'd come in early this morning, but after meeting Trudy, he needed a moment to think. He needed a strategy for dealing with her. The truth was, she was determined, opinionated and reminded him of Sue, the woman he'd almost married. There was nothing like young love to rip your heart out, he thought. Nothing like losing an unborn child to keep you from healing.

Shaking off the thoughts, Truman headed for his mother, and then later, after she was gone, he sipped a third cup of coffee. Finally, he glanced at his watch. "Thirty minutes." Long enough to communicate he was a busy guy.

Returning to his office, Truman traced his eyes over the files on his desk. "Where are they?" he suddenly whispered. As messy as things looked, he was flawlessly methodical. Capote and Dern hadn't picked up the files for the Glass Slipper case, which meant they should still be on his desk. They'd been right here, beneath the PR file that Trudy Busey...

"Oh, she's good," he muttered, realizing she'd stolen his files. And then he took long strides to the precinct's parking lot.

NOT ABOUT TO DWELL on the charged encounter with Truman Steele, Trudy curled a foot beneath her in the seat of his cruiser and delved into his files, scrutinizing photos of the most gorgeous shoes she'd ever seen. Steele was a good cop, she grudgingly admitted, jotting notes as she read statements taken from the theft victims, all of whom were nationally known women working in film, fashion, music or politics.

"These shoes are incredible," she whispered excitedly, leafing back through nearly a hundred publicity photos taken while the women were wearing them. There was a model on a runway, an actress traversing the red-carpeted entrance to the Oscars, an ex-first lady giving a luncheon speech. On their feet were everything from genie slippers to fabric-covered mules to zippered sandals with spiral heels. The NYPD hadn't released nearly this many photos to the press.

Assuring herself it was purely academic interest, Trudy started wondering how Truman had handled interviewing women who were so rich, beautiful and accomplished. Inhaling shakily, she tried not to think about how Truman's every breath and movement was underwritten by the taut thread of his sexuality. It was unbelievable, but nothing more than how he'd looked at her had made her shudder. His eyes were so much more than brown. They were hot honey that warmed, sweetened, promised...

She was almost glad for the distraction when the door against which she leaned was wrenched open. Reflexively, she grabbed the dashboard as her foot quickly gained purchase on the pavement. Scrambling from the car, she was preparing to defend herself when hands that should have been rough, but instead felt warm, strong and intriguing curled over her shoulders.

Suddenly, she could barely breathe. "Officer Steele?" Dammit, she'd been trying to keep an eye on the fire exit, so she could shove the stolen files under the seat when he came outside.

He yanked her toward him. "Expecting someone else?"

She swallowed hard as he slammed the car door. "I thought we were leaving?"

"Not yet."

Right now, he looked less the pretty-boy, more the cautious cop. Body heat seeped from his uniform shirt, and registering that their chests were just inches from touching, she felt her knees weaken. Oh, yes. It was definitely the wrong time to recall how his chest had looked in that photo—bare and smooth, just the way Trudy liked a man's chest to look, with pecs chiseled out of marble, the nipples hard. He was staring down at her with slanted eyes the color of undiluted bourbon when he lifted a finger, traced it lightly under her chin and used a thumb to turn her face more fully to his. "Look at me."

"Quit touching me and I will."

Male awareness filled his gaze. "Does that bother you?" he murmured. "Me touching you?"

"Of course it does." He dropped his hand, but not before the tips of her breasts tightened beneath her clothes. He couldn't see, of course. He didn't know. But as heat stained her cheeks, she wished they were upstairs again, with all those cops milling around instead of in this deserted garage.

"You stole my files."

Now that she'd successfully gotten rid of his hand, she vied for more. "Could you give me some breathing room?" Her back was flat against the car door, and the way he'd sandwiched her between his hard body and the metal was stealing her breath.

"What possessed you?"

She arched a brow. "Possessed? Must have been a demon."

"I'm beginning to believe it's just your personality."

"Don't worry," she returned dryly, pleased her voice was level. "I didn't read anything that would offend my finer sensibilities." Upstairs, the crime scene photos had sickened her more than she'd let on, and despite her usual fury over male protectiveness, she was strangely touched that Truman hadn't wanted her to see them.

"Are you really as hard as nails?"

"Of course not." Not usually. But she hadn't been prepared for what Truman Steele's photo couldn't divulge—his energy, core, essence, whatever you wanted to call it. "But I'm here to do a job."

"However dishonestly?"

"I'm a reporter." And she didn't intend to return to the *Milton Herald* where her lead stories had been even worse than this, involving runaway cows, backed-up town sewers and the occasional birth of twins. "What's dishonest is leaving a reporter in a parking lot while you pretend to be busy with work. Admit it, but weren't you eating another doughnut? Chocolate- or vanilla-filled?"

"Chocolate," he returned without hesitation.

"You kept me waiting intentionally."

"You stole those files."

She pointed to a napkin on the dashboard. "Someone was nice enough to give me a doughnut, too." She smiled. "And the files made for good reading." Seeing the furious glint in his eyes, she suspected she'd gone too far and tried to soften the blow with flattery. "My compliments. You do a very thorough interview."

"It's illegal to steal police files. I could run you back upstairs and book you."

"True. But Captain Coombs might be disappointed in my public relations article in the *News*."

"Blackmailer," he whispered. "You wouldn't."

She shrugged. "I'm interested in the Glass Slipper story. I'm hoping you'll talk to me. Off the record, if need be."

Grudging respect crept into eyes that were lingering too long at the open throat of her blouse, and when he leaned, as if to get a better look at her, his bemused lips seemed too close to her own. "*Talk* about my case?" he said. "I'd be *solving* it if I didn't have to chauffeur you around town."

She frowned. "Somebody else was given that case? Who?"

"Capote and Dern."

She'd heard of them. "They couldn't book loose paper with a stapler."

He looked pleased. "True."

"Did they get all your cases?"

He shook his head. "Only a few. The Glass Slipper victims don't like to feel there's no contact person available to them. Now," he continued, his voice turning grave, "have you read all my files?"

"Lunch at the Plaza," she returned, wishing everything about this man wasn't driving wind from her lungs with the force of a storm. "Wasn't that what you said I was dressed for? Maybe my interest in the shoes was merely fashion-oriented, did you think of that?"

Truman cursed. "You read every damn word."

"Steele," she said, liking the sound of his last name in her mouth. "To be perfectly honest, your timing was brilliant. Just as you got to the garage, I finished the last sentence."

"Get in, Trudy," he growled. "Mind if I call you Trudy?"

"Not so long as we don't have to shake hands." Body contact with Truman Steele might send her over the edge. She definitely liked how his hands looked. Large and long-fingered, with neat nails. Trying not to imagine how they might feel on her bare skin, she startled when he slammed the door, then scrambled inside and shut her own.

It was the perfect time to deliver the note she'd found under the windshield wiper. Leaning, she neatly tucked it into his uniform pocket, wishing she hadn't when she felt the hard muscular chest, his heart thumping under her fingertips.

"'Officer Steele,'" she quoted, "'I know you arrested me for drunk and disorderly conduct, but I need to talk to you. Let's have dinner soon. Best wishes, Candy.'"

His mouth was grim. "Stay out of my personal life."

"Personal life," she repeated, letting the irony speak for itself. "Do you often date women you arrest?"

Looking as if he'd like to arrest *her*, he said, "Never."

Biting back a laugh, she tucked her tongue into her cheek. She didn't know if she liked Truman Steele, per se. But she was enjoying their exchanges. Not that she'd deliver the dull story her boss expected. Like everyone, Truman had something to hide. Whatever it was, Trudy intended to find it.

3

DAYS AGO, WHEN TRUDY began delving into Truman's private life to enhance her article about the NYPD, she'd expected to discover secrets, but nothing like this. Crouching behind a bush in Bryant Park, she watched him leave the seventh sex toy shop this evening and head toward a triple-X marquee where a heavyset man with bulging biceps sat inside a smudgy glass booth, selling tickets. Most stores on the strip offered relatively tame sexy underwear and books, but one devoted itself to sinister zippered masks. Trudy shuddered, bringing up the camera slung around her neck and keeping Truman in the viewfinder as he changed his mind about the theatre and ducked into a dirty bookstore.

Times Square was hardly the red-light district it once was, but a few blocks away, here in Bryant Park, behind the New York Public Library's main branch, the streets remained dark and seedy. The night had turned too cool for the navy cardigan Trudy wore over a T-shirt and jeans, and the drizzle-dampened paper shopping bags that were brimming with purchases.

Ignoring catcalls from park dwellers, she snapped another photo, glad the headlights on Forty-first Street obscured the camera flash, her heart hurting as she considered how these pictures could ruin Truman's career. Maybe she should try talking to him. He had vices, yes. He was oversexed, yes. But didn't that mean he needed help?

So many here did. Over the past few nights, while tailing Truman, Trudy had interviewed people who called the park home, and she'd begun a heartbreaking, and she hoped, groundbreaking, story about their plight. As she listened, she could barely blink back tears, and most nights, she went home and wept. Sure, some people were hardened dopers, but others told stories of physical illness or emotional abuse, lost spouses, jobs and homes. The teens were the most gutwrenching. Unwanted and without opportunities, they felt their lives were over before they'd begun. Given a chance, Trudy knew they'd get on their feet.

Someone had to tell the public. As much as Trudy wanted to storm City Hall and demand intervention, it was her job to listen, care and write stories that mattered. Sure, she wanted the high profile leads—the lottery win, the Galapagos oil spill and the Glass Slipper—but it was people such as those she'd met in the park who truly motivated her.

"There you are," she murmured, her heart aching as Truman exited the book shop and darted toward the theater again. Despite her discovery of his double life, she couldn't help but notice he looked even better in street clothes than in his uniform. Her eyes skimmed down the chest-molding white T-shirt he wore beneath a windbreaker, loose black jeans faded to gray and stylish black workboots.

She tried not to think of all the hours he spent on corners talking to hookers. He didn't solely frequent shops in this part of town, either, but also those around

Grand Central Station. How had he wound up so lonely? Reduced to cruising?

Trudy wanted to look away, but it was her job to stare the truth boldly in the face. She shoved the two shopping bags between her legs and hoped none of the drug dealers drifting through the unlit expanse of the park would steal them. Since most had come to know her name when she'd interviewed them, she doubted they would.

"The NYPD's poster boy," she whispered, wishing Truman's wasn't the tragic story of a cop who'd crossed the line. She'd sensed he was more sexual than most men, but who could have guessed he spent every night here? It had cost a month's salary, but Trudy had spent heavily in the shops he frequented, and although she'd never been inside such stores before, she'd hit pay dirt. When she spent money, clerks talked. After scrutinizing the plainclothes NYPD photo she'd used to identify Truman, they'd assured her he was a regular customer. Shivering against the damp air, she watched him stop under the lurid marquee to talk to two shady characters.

By day he seemed so normal. After discovering his double life, Trudy had increased her interpersonal efforts during their drive-alongs, acting friendly and getting him to talk. He presented himself as all-American. As a sports fan who'd been a good student and active in school. He volunteered for the D.A.R.E. program, talking to youngsters about not using drugs, and he loved his parents and brothers, spending much of his recreational time with them. Before she discovered his secret life, Trudy had begun to consider...

Sleeping with him? Trudy pushed away the thought.

She had to concentrate on her job. By day, she prayed Truman would never suspect she was following him by night. Unfortunately, as she toured the city with him, she kept wanting to forget the lurid places she watched him visit when he was off the clock.

The Truman she was coming to know by day had become as amiable as she. Unlike her father and brothers, he made her feel worthy of undivided attention. Her carefully erected guard had started to crumble. She'd found herself rediscovering a city both she and Truman loved, and she enjoyed seeing it through the sharp eyes of a native, one who gladly answered all her questions about police life.

Snapping another picture, she wondered when the long hours had finally gotten to Truman, when he'd given up on girlfriends who couldn't understand the stresses of his profession. Only aching loneliness could have forced him to this forbidden part of the city where he spent hours exhausting his physical needs. How desperate he must feel, Trudy thought, how hungry for sexual release.

Strangely, she could identify. Oh, not with what Truman Steele had been reduced to, but with the edgy, pent-up need and loneliness that felt so empty it hurt. Some nights, alone in bed, the want of a partner gnawed at her soul. Cravings made her burn. Frustrated and unsatisfied, she tossed and turned. She'd never really felt a man's greedy hands on her body, nor surrendered to the ultimate pleasure only a man could bring.

Instead she'd ignored men for years, assuring herself there'd be time for that part of her life once she was established in the news world. Only then would she allow herself a lover. But she was almost established now, wasn't she? And for the male body, she had the same curiosity that drove her at work....

Heat flushed her face. Truman Steele was so potent, virile and male that, unbidden, her breath quickened. He needed a woman, and suddenly, it didn't seem fair that he take his comfort from strangers. She'd begun thinking about him all the time. At home, she'd stare curiously at the photos she'd taken of him, or at the bare-chested photo of him in his patrol car. Shopping in these stores hadn't helped. Amidst the tacky items, Trudy had discovered some that intrigued her, and the purchases had begun to fuel wild, hot fantasies....

This morning, she'd given in to temptation. In the deli where she bought milk, she'd picked up batteries, blushing furiously as she paid, as if the clerk might read her mind and realize she planned to try one of the devices she'd bought. It was wicked. Probably perverse. But she just couldn't help herself. Anytime she imagined wild, uncontrolled vibrations against her flesh, sensual pleasure burst through her...

Tonight, while digging for information about Truman, she'd bought a flesh-colored vibrator fashioned in the shape of a penis. She simply couldn't believe she'd done so. If she wasn't here on official business for the *News*, she'd be mortified. As the clerk handed her the package, she realized her earlier trip to the deli wasn't even necessary. Batteries were included. Now Trudy licked dry lips, thinking that maybe tonight, maybe after she got home...

She shouldn't have let her mind wander! She'd lost sight of Truman! Frustrated, she whirled just as she heard his voice call from the darkness. "Trudy? Is that you? What are you doing out here?"

He was behind her! Apparently he'd passed the theater and crossed the street, doubling back when he noticed her. Had he seen her photographing porn shops? She hoped not! He was still a half block away. Trying not to look suspicious, she circled the bush she'd crouched behind, as well as a foot-high iron rail, then stepped onto the sidewalk, her mind racing with possible explanations for her presence.

Drizzle had done marvelous things for his hair, defining the long strands, pasting them against his cheeks and neck. His shirt was so tight, that beneath the pull of cotton, she could see hardened nipples. Instinctively, she edged away from her shopping bags. *Please,* she thought, doing a mental inventory. *Don't let him look inside.* In addition to the vibrator, there were French ticklers, love oils and a special humidifier that dispensed something called "aphrodisiac steam."

He waved. "What are you doing here?" he repeated amicably.

At least the bags wouldn't give her away, since the stores didn't have logos and were of plain brown paper. "Shopping!" she called, lifting the camera around her neck. "And I wanted to get some night shots of Times Square. It's changed so much since the Disney Store moved there, don't you think?"

"They've really cleaned up the area," he agreed.

Shaking her head ruefully, she tried to look sheepish. "I guess I got carried away. I wound up straying from the beaten path."

He jerked his chin upward in a New Yorker's version of a nod. "Did you take the subway?"

He was so nonchalant that, moments before, he could have been standing outside *The Lion King,* not a movie called *Suzie Licks my Boots.* Trudy inhaled sharply, sensing a sudden movement behind her. Turning, her eyes landed in the park where streetlights didn't penetrate. Just as her eyes focused closer, air swished on either side of her. She gasped, "My bags!"

As they were whisked from the pavement, she glimpsed the snatcher—a white kid on a graffiti-covered skateboard. He was about fourteen, with short pink hair and beaded necklaces that jangled against his chest as he turned away. He was in her face one second, gone the next. "Wait! You can't take those!"

But he was gone, airborne as he hopped the railing, clutching a bag in each hand, his skateboard clinging to his sneakers as if glued to them, unaffected by gravity. The rollers slammed down hard as the board hit concrete, then he pumped with a foot. As he glided through the park, the receding sound of rollers seemed loud in the still night, despite the heavy traffic. Truman caught up to her, then passed at a run, easily hurdling the rail, yelling, "You okay?"

"I'm not hurt! Forget about the bags!"

"Don't worry, I'll be right back. I'll get them!"

Truman was fast and graceful, running like a sleek animal with the wind in his damp hair until the darkness of the park swallowed him. Trudy realized she'd frozen on the sidewalk, and that Truman was still chasing the kid, who'd clearly intended to cut through the park and go east on Forty-second Street toward Fifth Avenue. Truman couldn't retrieve the bags! She'd sooner die that have him see what was inside. The bags were wet from the rain, too! What if they ripped and all those love oils and French ticklers scattered onto the sidewalk?

Her face flaming, Trudy bolted down Forty-first Street, her sneakered feet pounding the cement. Instead of cutting through the park, she ran along the shadowy stone facade of the massive library. She had to reach Fifth Avenue before Truman. If the kid ran south, maybe she'd catch him first. By not cutting through the park, she was gaining leverage.

Please, she thought. *Let me get those bags before Truman.*

AS HE RAN, TRUMAN focused on the kid's back and wished Trudy hadn't gotten turned around in such a bad neighborhood. She could have gotten hurt. Fortunately, this guy was just a punk. He had pink hair and was wearing more necklaces than you'd find in a jewelry store. He was on a skateboard, though, so catching him was a pain. Panting as he weaved around people on the sidewalk, Truman wished he'd brought a weapon, just in case, but when he was off-duty, he rarely carried.

"Stop," he shouted. "Put down the bags."

"Those are Trudy's bags!" someone yelled as he neared the entrance to the library.

Who out here knew Trudy? Most of the guys in the park were drug dealers, but there was no time to reason it out. "Lucky me," Truman whispered as the kid circled the corner onto Fifth Avenue and hopped off the skateboard. Stilling the rollers with his hand, he vanished up the library steps on foot, hauling the bags. Away from the street, it was dark, and the kid was hoping Truman would continue running and assume he'd lost his quarry in the crowds.

The kid was hiding—either behind one of the columns near the library's brass revolving doors, or behind one of two mammoth marble lions. Stately, the lions were perched on their haunches halfway up the wide stone steps, guarding the library like sentinels, their huge paws extended and long manes flowing.

Pausing to catch his breath, Truman glanced around, but didn't see Trudy. He'd hated leaving her at the south entrance of Bryant Park. It was dark there, not that the library steps were any better lit. Squinting into inky blackness, he moved slowly upward, keeping his eyes peeled, a slight smile curling his lips.

The shopping bags had bogged the kid down. The bags looked heavy, too. *It's a wonder*, Truman thought, shaking his head, *the damage women can do when they shop.* But what stores were in the neighborhood? He frowned. Bloomingdale's was on the East Side, Barneys was downtown, and Agnès B. was in Soho. The Warner Brothers and Disney stores, he realized, his smile broadening. They were running sales. No doubt, Trudy was getting a head start on Christmas, buying stuff for the four nephews she'd mentioned during their ride-alongs.

Strangely, she'd turned out to be the type. After that first rocky encounter, she'd started changing for no reason Truman could fathom. She'd begun trying to get to know him, and he'd become more curious about her, too. Despite her ambition, and the fact that her brothers were the heirs apparent to her father's newspaper, she loved them. Both were married, each with toddlers, all little boys...

"Stealing kids' Christmas presents," Truman muttered with disgust as he edged stealthily around the paw of a lion. Well, he'd retrieve the gifts. The punk was just on the other side of the statue. Truman tilted his head to listen, then heard a low, mechanical hum.

He almost laughed. The skateboarder's jostling had caused one of the toys Trudy had bought the kids to switch on. Whatever it was, it was battery-operated. Now there was a rustle of paper. The guy was reaching into the bag, trying to turn off the toy.

"I hear you," Truman singsonged. Dodging around the lion, he feinted left, then doubled back, changing directions once more. The confused teenager barreled into him, nearly knocking him down, and Truman grabbed the bags. "Here. Why don't I take those?"

"Believe me," muttered the teen over his shoulder, grabbing his skateboard and running down the steps, "You can have them. I don't want that kind of stuff!"

Truman chuckled, imagining the kid opening the bags and examining his haul—only to realize he'd stolen two bags of T-shirts, Pokémon toys, Batmobiles and the like. Relieved, he saw Trudy rounding the corner and lifted the bags. "Got them!"

Something had definitely gotten jostled. It was too dark to see, but Truman dug a hand into one of the bags until his fingers locked around whatever was vibrating. Lifting it from the bag, he squinted at the object. It was about six inches long and about two inches thick at the base. "Some kind of fighter jet," he supposed. "Or an alien rocket ship." Yeah. It looked like one of those flesh-colored toys that came with a paint set, so you could decorate it yourself. Usually, the colors were green and black, for camouflage. When they were kids, his brother Sully used to love this stuff.

Still fiddling with the gizmo, he mistook the approaching footsteps for Trudy's and glanced up. "Hey, what's this thing anyway?" he asked, staring into the dark. "One of those remote-control rockets?"

"Them's Trudy's," a deep male voice said. "Don't you be messing with Trudy's bags, boy. You give them back."

"What?" Truman stepped toward the light, simultaneously realizing that the base of the toy twisted, and that a huge black man was in front of him. No wonder he hadn't seen him. The man's skin was the exact color of the darkness.

"Don't you be messing with Trudy," he said again.

The second before the man's fist connected with his jaw, Truman gasped. It was impossible, but all at once, he realized he was gripping a *penis!* Staring in shock, his first thought was that he wasn't gay, so this couldn't be happening. His second was that this wasn't an appropriate gift for Trudy's nephews. His third was that Trudy Busey had been down here, buying herself a vibrator.

"Wait, Leon! Don't hit him! He's a friend!"

But Trudy's voice came too late. Shock had left Truman defenseless, and when Leon's next punch slammed his temple, everything went black.

"HOLD STILL," TRUDY whispered.

Truman winced. He wasn't sure, but thought she was smoothing his hair. Whatever she was doing, it felt like heaven. "Where am I?" he asked, his voice hoarse, his head pounding.

"My apartment."

Something about his jaw didn't feel right, and it took him a minute to register that the acrid taste, now thankfully dissolving, had probably been blood. Carefully, he tried opening his eyes, but only one opened all the way. The other slit open just enough to view a slice of skyline through a window. He recognized a green neon burger as that which hung above Billy's Burgers on the corner of Sixth and Thirteenth.

So, that's where she lived. He'd been curious, and he could have found out easily since he was a cop, but he'd decided to wait, mostly because he'd imagined winding up here some night after dinner and a movie, if the pleasant conversation they were sharing in the patrol car continued. Of course, she also seemed off-limits. Truman needed a wife, and he'd prefer to marry someone he could safely divorce after they divvied up the lottery win. Groaning, he muttered, "You have any aspirin?"

"Tylenol."

"I'm not picky. I could use some water, too. A shot of whiskey wouldn't be bad, either."

She frowned apologetically. "I might have blackberry wine."

Somehow, that didn't surprise him. The mere thought turned his stomach. The stuff probably tasted like cough syrup. "Thanks, but I'll pass. Water'll be fine."

"Here. Before I go..." He inhaled sharply as she tugged the T-shirt from his waistband, her palms smoothing over his ribs and nipples as she pushed it up, easing it over his head. Putting the shirt aside, she gently pressed a scrape on his shoulder with her fingertips. "This looks terrible."

The way she was touching it made it feel better.

"Wait here."

Hearing her footsteps recede, he concentrated on his aches and pains. Just as he decided he hadn't broken anything, he realized he was lying on her futon, and that it was unfolded, like a double bed. It smelled of her, too—soft, floral, feminine. Funny, he thought, allowing himself to drift, ever since his mother won the lotto, he'd quit looking at women. Usually the world seemed full of them. Tall and short. Slender and voluptuous. But just a day after his mother had challenged him and his brothers to find brides, he'd met Trudy...

The melee at the library crowded into his consciousness. Whoever Leon was, he'd been a huge sucker. He'd had friends, too. Opening his eyes again, Truman realized Trudy had returned, and he let her lift his head, surprised at how tender her palm felt, circling his neck and cupping it. Emotion twisted inside him, sharp and unexpected. He hadn't been touched this tenderly by anyone except his mother, not even Sue. He swallowed the Tylenol, shook his head to clear it of confusion, then squinted at Trudy. "How'd I get here, anyway?"

"Leon and Alfredo. Alfredo's got a car." Trudy was hovering above him, her face drawn and pale as she eyed him. Not only did she look as if she felt personally responsible for his injuries, she was glancing anxiously over her shoulder, looking around her apartment as if wishing she could have taken him somewhere else. He supposed it was because so many Manhattan apartments were in ancient buildings and left something to be desired. Just as Truman started to survey his surroundings, Trudy stepped in front of him, as if to block his view.

"Leon was sorry he hit you," she said. "He asked me to tell you that."

With a grunt, Truman bunched some pillows behind him and edged upward, resting his back against the wall. Once he was sitting up, his mind felt clearer. His eyebrows furrowing, he touched a sore placed at his temple and said, "Mind if I ask how a sweet girl like you happens to know a rough character like Leon?"

Along with the Tylenol, she'd returned with alcohol and cotton, and now she uncapped the bottle. Tilting it, she soaked the cotton, then whispered, "This is going to hurt."

"Don't sidestep," he warned. "I want to know about Leon."

"I'm not sidestepping," she defended. "I'm doctoring."

If he hadn't met her friends, he wouldn't need doctoring, but she looked so worried that he refrained from mentioning it. He felt her clean a wound with gentle swipes. She drew a breath through clenched teeth as she worked and held it, as if she, not he, were the patient. "About Leon," she finally said. "He's really a nice guy. Ever since he got out of Rikers last month, he's been living in the park, so I interviewed him." She sighed apologetically. "I'm sorry, Truman. Leon took a shine to me when I told him he'd be central in my in-depth piece about the homeless in Bryant Park."

Somehow, that surprised him. He didn't know much

about how reporters worked. "You have other stories?"

She looked incredulous. "Of course. Some are assigned. Others I'm creating, hoping to pitch them to Dimi. The people down there really need to be heard," she said with quiet passion. "And Leon's afraid something might happen to me before I can get the *News* to print his statement."

Truman realized she'd sidetracked him again. Nothing more than her eyes could have that effect. "Did you say Rikers?" he repeated levelly. "As in Island? The prison?"

She nodded. "I tried to get Alfredo to stop at Beth Israel hospital," she explained reasonably, "but when Leon found out you were a cop, he was afraid they'd get into trouble. He insisted you come here. I was getting ready to call an ambulance."

"I'm fine," he managed. He'd taken more knocks roughhousing with his brothers. She didn't look convinced, so he added, "Really, Trudy. My brothers have done worse."

She laughed softly, and he realized she was thinking of her own. "I believe you. Bob and Ed used to have some doozies." Despite that, she sobered and peered at him a long moment, her eyebrows knitting, the concern in her blue eyes touching him. "Still...you don't look okay."

"Leon," he said simply.

"Well," she defended, "I know what you're thinking, but Leon's just had some tough luck. He's from horrible projects in the Bronx, and when he was younger, peer pressure got to him. There wasn't enough money at home, and he wound up doing time for robbing apartments. He could go back to that, you know," she assured stridently, "but he knows that's the easy way out. He's trying to make enough money to get off the street." Truman's sharp gasp stopped her. "Sorry," she murmured.

"It's okay," he assured as she resumed, dabbing what felt like a paper cut near his left eye. He couldn't stop from adding, "My main complaint's that the smell of alcohol overwhelms the scent that belongs to you." The scent of her skin, hair and bed were driving him crazy.

He was glad to see her look so pleased. "Really?"

"Really." Truman's groin tightened. He'd never seen her in jeans, only suits, and a wave of heat suffused him as he took in skin that glowed from the drizzle outside. Her damp T-shirt clung, hugging small, firm breasts so tightly that he'd have thought her braless, if not for the fact that he could make out straps. He knew he should distract himself before he got aroused, but she kept slowly, tenderly probing the flesh of wounds that weren't nearly as debilitating as she seemed to want to pretend. In fact, from how his face felt, he was sure the injuries were superficial. By tomorrow, no one would notice. He'd gotten a lump on the back of his head from hitting the library steps after Leon decked him. That's what had knocked him out.

Before he thought it through, Truman caught her hand, sliding his thumb into the hollow of her palm. As he considered pulling her down on top of him, he noticed how her eyes widened and knew he'd been right. She wanted him. Reaching, he smoothed away drops of warm rain water that had caught on her skin, his senses heightening. As the cobwebs cleared, his mind

sharpened, focusing. More of the evening came back—
the content of those shopping bags, how his fingers
had clutched around a...

He blinked, feeling wide-awake.

Withdrawing his hand, he forced himself to appear
relaxed. Evening his breath, he let her administer to his
wounds again while he surreptitiously scrutinized the
tiny studio. It was the kind of apartment that, with city
prices, went for over a thousand dollars a month despite its scant five-hundred square feet. A tiny kitchen,
no larger than a bus bathroom, opened off a main
room, and the bath wasn't any bigger.

His gaze settled on a black feather boa she'd draped
over a chair, then traveled to a table. Years of training
kept him from reacting visibly as he took in the handcuffs, edible panties and fur G-string. By the time his
eyes landed on an unopened package of batteries, it
took zero imagination to figure out why she'd bought
them. Apparently tonight wasn't the first night Trudy
had gone shopping in the red-light district.

Thick bands slowly tightened around his ribs. No
wonder she was so nervous about him seeing her living space. Oh, he'd gotten the impression that she was
an avoider when it came to relationships. She was ambitious, afraid a man would get in the way of her work.
But why would a woman like her settle for mechanical
devices? She could have anyone!

His jeans pulled with the onslaught of unwanted desire, and he drew a breath through his teeth as the erection he couldn't stop nudged his zipper. He kept seeing Trudy, lying on her back, wearing nothing but that
feather boa, her creamy legs spread and her face
flushed with passion. Truman's breath was so shallow

his lungs hurt. Suddenly, he grabbed her hand again. Using it for leverage, he abruptly swung his legs over the edge of the futon and sat up. Maybe that would help.

Trudy's voice was strained. "You okay?"

"Just need to sit up," he managed gruffly. She knew damn well he'd seen the prizes she'd brought home.

She was standing next to him, leaning forward in a way that made her look perched on her tiptoes, as if she was trying to use her slender body to shield him from seeing her apartment. Slowly, with shaking hands, she put the cotton and alcohol on a table...right next to the device Truman had been holding at the library.

He glanced at her, his heart doing a wild, crazy flip-flop. Her face was dewy from the night, pink with heat, her shirt so damp he could make out everything beneath. Dammit, somebody had to say something. "Don't worry," he managed, not wanting her to be embarrassed. He took a deep breath only to have her scent fill his lungs. "Really Trudy, what you've got here is nothing I haven't seen before."

That seemed to throw her off. Her lips parted in surprise. "You don't think I, uh, wanted these things for..." Pausing, she became too embarrassed to continue, and when she spoke again, her voice was almost shaking. "For my own, uh..."

He fought it, but the word came out deep and husky. "Pleasure?" he supplied.

Trudy looked mortified. "No! You've got this all wrong..."

"Don't worry," he assured gently. "I'm not the type to pass judgment." He thought about how tough she tried to seem, how ambitious, how married to her work... "We all get lonely," he continued, his fingers itching to touch her, his palms turning damp with the need. "I've been a cop a long time. I've seen just about everything, Trudy."

She drew an audible breath, and the way her chest was heaving, accentuating handfuls of firm, sweet breasts, he wished she wasn't standing quite so close. "These things, uh, aren't mine," she said. "I mean, they're not for..."

This was a standard move when people were guilty. "You want to turn things around because you're embarrassed, but there's no need—"

"*I'm* not embarrassed!"

He murmured, "People have needs."

She looked trapped. "I don't," she defended.

"Trudy, you're aching for a man." She'd cut herself off, denying natural desires. Her career was just an excuse. He knew her avoidance ran deeper. Some men became cops because they were macho. Others because they hated bad guys. Truman liked to know what made people tick. And right now, he wanted to know what made Trudy tick. Oh, he was aroused. She'd been tempting him for days, and now they were alone in her tiny apartment, surrounded by every sex toy known to man. How could he resist? But sex would never be enough. It was Trudy's psyche he wanted. She was a complicated woman. And he was a complicated man.

"You're the one who spends all your time down there," she whispered, her imploring eyes willing him to understand.

He squinted. "In Times Square?"

Her lips parted beseechingly, making him want to

plumb their depths. She pointed upward, and his eyes followed. He hadn't noticed before, but she'd strung a clothesline across the room. Photos—some black and white, some color—hung from a line by pins. Many were of street people—tragic, heart-wrenching photos—but there were also about twenty pictures of him.

His jaw slackened. She'd photographed him standing outside every dirty movie theater in the city. "You think I..." He grasped her wrist, drawing her beside him on the futon with the need to explain. A second too late, he realized he'd brought her hand to his upper thigh. The pulse beating at her wrist was thumping hard, and their thighs were touching.

"I've been following you," she explained hurriedly, licking against the dryness of her lips, her eyes flicking to where he held her wrist against his tensed thigh. "I shouldn't have. But I did. I've seen all the places where you..."

Did she really think he was paying for peep shows? "You were following me? At night?"

"Yes. And I saw..."

He could well imagine. Anger came after surprise. "What gave you the right to check up on me, Trudy?"

She looked both offended and guilty. "I'm a reporter."

One who thought he was a sex pervert. Truman glanced slowly around the room. Closer scrutiny revealed the items were new, never used. "And you bought all this stuff...?"

Color was flooding her face, and she was too embarrassed to move her hand from his thigh even though she obviously wanted to. But she was also excited.

Heaven help him, but her pulse was vibrating against his fingertips.

"I went into the stores you, uh, frequent..."

"And bought these things? So clerks would talk?"

"I'm sorry," she rushed on, looking relieved that he understood. "I asked questions, but the proprietors didn't know you're a cop. You've got to believe me, Truman," she implored. "This stuff wasn't for me...."

His eyes settled on the batteries again. No doubt, things were as she said. But she was curious, and later, after she'd gotten home, she'd begun to wonder...

His eyes slid to the pictures again, and as much as he hated doing this, he pointed. "Trudy, you see those two guys? And those two women?" He pointed at two blondes in fishnets and miniskirts.

She nodded. "Yes. Yes, I'm afraid I do, Truman."

"They're vice cops. We went to the academy together."

She stared at him a long moment, then simply said, "No, oh no," her blush deepening as the truth sank in.

"Determined to make something more out of a boring PR piece, you followed me, huh?" Anger and desire tying him in knots, Truman forced himself to continue. "You thought you discovered my secret life. Were you going to publish that I was a pervert?"

"At first," she admitted quickly. "But then I thought I'd talk to you. I figured you needed help..."

As good a cop as he was, he should have been prepared for this, and under any other circumstances he'd have laughed. But she'd been so nice in the cruiser, so curious about him. "You played me," he whispered softly.

"At first," she said, her eyes asking him to go easy on

her. "But then, I started having a good time with you, riding around the city. I just thought...you were lonely."

"Enough to go to Times Square for a woman?" Was she out of her mind?

"I thought you'd call Candy first," she conceded. "I mean, she leaves all those notes under your windshield wipers."

Candy? "I arrested her once on a drunk, disorderly charge. That's all." Truman could only shake his head. What kind of man did she think he was? He was offended, aroused, and yet strangely touched, since Trudy was the sort of woman who spent her evenings interviewing homeless people and trying to save men she thought might be sex perverts. "Trudy," he said simply.

She looked expectant, even hopeful, as if he'd offer some way out of the bind she was in. "Yes?"

He pointed toward a photo of a movie marquee, reading the title. *"Suzie Licks my Boots."*

She gasped, her face lighting up, then she groaned. "The Glass Slipper case?"

"I figure the perpetrator is a foot fetishist. One of those guys who can't..." He paused a beat before going on. "Who can't be fully satisfied unless he's thinking about a woman's feet."

Trudy showed all the subtle signs of a woman whose brain was working overtime: her head tilted slightly, her eyes narrowed almost imperceptibly. "Didn't Ivana Trump, Donald's wife, once have a pair of shoes stolen by a foot fetishist?"

Truman nodded. "Yeah. In the eighties."

"I remember the article," she said, her color returning to normal as she trained her mind on the case. "Did you question the man who did that?"

"He's the first person I talked to. He couldn't have been in town during one of the thefts."

"You know the exact time the shoes were stolen?"

"Not in all the thefts, but in a couple of them. Anyway, I'm checking out the shops. The owners think I'm trying to sell homemade video movies that feature women's shoes."

"I knew there was something strange about those pictures," Trudy mused, her voice catching. "I kept coming back to them, feeling that I was wrong about something."

"Yeah." He stared at her. "Me. As a sex deviant."

But suddenly, it didn't matter. The pink color, brought by the evening's exertion was staining Trudy's cheeks, making her look lovely, and her skin was glowing with night dew. Once more, his eyes flitted around the room, taking in the toys, and he imagined her wearing nothing but that feather boa.

When his eyes sought hers again, she quickly averted her gaze. "Your face looks better," she managed, her voice strained with what he hoped was desire. "Can I get you some coffee? Or flavored seltzer?"

Given how enticing she looked, he decided he wasn't going anywhere else tonight. "What flavor?"

"Raspberry, I think."

"Words like *think* bother me, Trudy."

She shot him a look of worried apology. "They do?"

He nodded slowly. "I'd rather go for a sure thing."

Her eyes slid away. Together, they took in the fur panties, feather boa, handcuffs and other sundries. And then Trudy looked him square in the eye and whispered, "Me, too, Truman."

4

TRUDY WAS NEVER SO TORN as when the phone rang. Truman was about to initiate her into sex, but what if the caller was a source with a hot tip? Or Dimi, finally giving her the dynamite lead he kept promising? Swallowing with difficulty and not taking her eyes off Truman, she murmured, "I'm so sorry," and lifted the cordless, trying to ignore his disappointment and the persistent pressure of his thigh against hers. "Busey speaking."

"Is everything okay? You sound funny. Did I wake you?"

Dad. She cursed herself for answering. He always assumed she was at home alone and in bed by ten, and as much as Trudy hated admitting it, this was the first time he hadn't been right. "I'm great." Pride compelled her to add, "But I was just on my way out. Dimi called with a lead."

"I'm sure he did, Trudy, but you're only twenty-eight. And you're in a big city..."

"Where I've lived for seven years." Wincing, she realized he suspected Dimi hadn't really called, and while he hadn't meant to hurt her, his placating tone burned like salt in a wound, a sore reminder of Scott Smith-Sanker's gloating smiles whenever Dimi assigned her another human-interest story. Her mind flashed on her last Christmas visit. She'd arrived home wearing black wraparound shades and a calf-length leather coat that had cost too much of her salary, clothes she hadn't cared about but had bought because she wanted her family to acknowledge she'd conquered the nation's toughest city. *You look so hip, sweetie,* Ed's wife had patronized, in a way that made Trudy sound eight years old, not twenty-eight.

Très chic, Trudy's other sister-in-law had interjected. Trudy could still hear Ed saying, *I loved that bit you did on the ice sculptures in front of Rockefeller Center, kiddo.* And Bob adding, *Interviewing tourists about their impressions of New York holiday decorations was knockout stuff, sis.*

Right, Trudy thought ruefully. Those stories were a travesty when there was so much important work to be done. Glancing toward the photos of the homeless, she sighed. She could have used the *News*'s darkroom, but feared Dimi would see the photos and give the story to Scott. She'd call herself paranoid, but that very thing had happened two months ago when she'd prepared to pitch a story about chemical waste. It wasn't fair. Why couldn't somebody believe in her?

The only saving grace was knowing she could win a Pulitzer and her father and brothers would still address her with the same condescension. Feeling light years away from the stories she was born to tell, she turned her eyes to the pictures of Truman, then the racy items in the room. Her heart thudded dully against her ribs. Was another of her dreams, one of sexual fulfillment, about to come true?

Looking at Truman, Trudy knew she could do far worse. He'd been so sweet. He didn't want her to be embarrassed, so he'd pretended not to notice she'd been interested in all these love toys. Her knees weakening, she managed to say, "Dad, I'm busy. I've got to go."

"Well, before you do, I called to say Ed, Bob and I are coming to New York next weekend for the annual Newsprint Media Conference. We know you're not registering, due to that busy schedule of yours, but we're hoping to see you for dinner Saturday night." He quickly added, "If you can fit us in."

Once more, he was placating her. "I'll look forward to it," she said, guilt softening her tone, since even though she loved her family members, she dreaded entertaining them.

"Well, you know Ed's spent time in the city, but he said he'd let you pick the restaurant this time."

"How nice of him." Because Ed had spent a summer after college waiting tables here and broadening his horizons, he always played the expert. Funny, she thought. Her brothers were only two and four years older than she, and yet they seemed middle-aged, married with kids, content to run the family paper. Well, no doubt something would go wrong at whatever restaurant she chose, and Ed would imply he would have picked a better one.

"Are Kate and Sherry coming?" she asked, her mind turning to the S.I.L.'s whom her father wouldn't think to mention, since he'd consider them tag-alongs.

"Are you kidding? The wives wouldn't miss clothes shopping in New York for the world. We've got one sitter lined up to watch all four of your nephews."

"Great," Trudy said, mustering enthusiasm. Quickly saying goodbye, she put down the phone and turned to Truman, feeling uncomfortably conscious of his closeness. Everything felt more intimate now that he'd overheard the conversation with her father. Without intending to, he'd stepped into the minefield of her emotional life. When his penetrating, intense brown eyes fixed on hers, they seemed to say he'd liked seeing another side of her.

Wanting to talk about anything other than her family, she flicked her eyes over his face, saying the first thing that came to mind. "Your eyes are so unusual."

A teasing smile played on his lips. "I'm not used to women commenting on my eyes."

She narrowed hers. "I doubt that, Truman."

He shrugged, the smile warming his features. "What do you mean? Unusual?"

"Now you're fishing for compliments."

"True," he admitted.

There was no hint he shared the patronizing attitude she'd grown up with. No, his honeyed eyes were only hungry, sharpened by male awareness. "They're interesting," she explained. "Slanted." She chuckled playfully, suspecting he'd kept more women than her up late at night, fantasizing about him, and she noted that the gash at his temple didn't detract from his good looks in the least, no more than the nasty scrape on his shoulder. "Surely you look in mirrors."

He was still smiling. "Only when I cut myself shaving."

It was probably the truth. He was a dedicated patrolman, one without time for frivolity, much less vanity. But the fact remained. The tilt of those eyes was compelling. The lids stayed at half-mast as if he were constantly anticipating satisfaction. Trudy's throat tightened. The air between them was so charged she could barely breathe.

She cleared her throat, wondering what to say next, and unable to stand the tension, settled on, "Where were we?"

He glanced briefly at the phone, and she was glad when he changed his mind about addressing what he'd overheard. His lips parted a fraction to expose straight, gleaming teeth. "I think—" His voice lowered. "You were about to pursue a hot lead, Trudy."

"Sorry for the interruption," she apologized, meeting his gaze and hoping she looked more in control than she felt. "I usually give hot leads my full attention."

He nodded, eyes sparkling. "You like to make sure you follow stories through to the end?"

"The important ones, anyway."

"Am I an important one, Trudy?"

Yes. There was no denying he was getting to her. "That remains to be seen, doesn't it?"

"When you're on a story," he murmured, skating a finger from her wrist up her bare arm, "which do you like best?" The finger settled on her shoulder. "The beginning? The middle?" She sucked in a breath as the finger slid under the collar of her T-shirt. "Or the end?"

It was the wrong time to admit she'd never actually made it all the way to the end. Knowing she was silently saying she'd make love with him, she suddenly couldn't believe any of this was happening. "I can't answer that," she managed breathlessly. "Not until this particular story's over, can I?"

"Guess not. So we'd better get busy. I want an answer."

The night flashed before her eyes—spying on Truman in Bryant Park, trying to stop Leon from punching him, driving him to her apartment in Alfredo's car. What a strange night. And yet it seemed so right. A turbulent night for a turbulent couple. She wondered if turbulence would describe what was about to happen between them in bed.

"As it turns out," he continued, the steady pressure of his thigh against hers making her lose her mind, "I got a hot lead tonight, too."

She melted as the finger began stroking her collarbone, and her heart stuttered as he drew her against him. Leaning back her head to accept a kiss, she whispered, "You did, Truman?"

Nodding, he reached and flicked off the light, so only the faint glow of streetlamps filtered through the curtains, then he slid a thumb down her cheek, resting the pad in the dip of her chin. Slowly, he traced the tip over her lower lip, brushing to and fro before repeatedly circling the mouth that his own intended to claim.

"I'm always interested in a hot lead," she assured, glad she was sitting down since, given the tender way he was touching her, her legs wouldn't have supported her. "What did your source say, Truman?"

His husky voice, like the thumb on her lip, sent a thrill rippling through her blood. "That we're going to be explosive in bed."

The thumb dipped then, tracing a ridge of lower teeth before pressing inside. As it withdrew, her lips closed instinctually, her teeth grazing the pad while her tongue explored it. Her cheeks pulled to suckle, her lips kissed the tip. "This source is reliable?" she managed on a barely concealed pant when his thumb, now damp, was once more resting on her lip.

"He never fails."

"Very sure of himself," she commented.

"Completely."

"I'll trust you on this, Truman."

He didn't seem to have heard. "You're so pretty, Trudy."

Because she'd spent days imagining him in a state of lonely desperation, she'd envisioned him taking her quickly and fiercely, driven by dark, primitive forces he couldn't harness. Instead, he warned her, coming closer, simply saying, "I'm going to kiss you now, Trudy. Is that okay with you?"

"I think I can handle that." Actually, she wasn't nearly as sure as she sounded.

Remarkably restrained lips fitted to hers, testing the contours of her mouth, varying pressure and bringing new rushes of delight with each slight readjustment. By slow, stealthy degrees, Truman found the touch she most craved, and by the time he did, their lips were tightly locked, having snapped perfectly together in pure possessive pleasure.

By then, her heart was thudding against her ribs, and his hands had swept around her back while hers landed above his knees. Bracing herself against hard thighs, she felt his muscles flexing beneath her palms. As he deepened the pressure of the kiss, she was suddenly powerless but to glide her hands higher...then higher still.

Sensing their direction, Truman groaned, his mouth slackening against hers before a renewed onslaught made the kiss burst with new heat. A liquid, searing tongue shot between her lips, playfully gliding along-side hers, then tangled and finally darted in rhythm, swiftly dueling with hers as he sought to conquer and make her yield.

She'd fought men off for years, but imagining Truman's unusual appetite for sex had aroused her immeasurably. Now Trudy couldn't wait to surrender...to let him take what so many others had wanted so badly. She wanted him to succeed where others had failed. Not to be undone by her own lack of confidence, she tightened her grip on his thighs, protesting on a sigh when his mouth left hers. "No," she murmured. "Don't quit kissing me, Truman."

"I won't," he assured, easing the T-shirt over her head, just as she had his. A gasp tore from her throat. She had to cover herself! She'd forgotten! She'd worn underwear she'd bought from a sex shop while following Truman! How could she have done this?

Embarrassed heat flooded her. It was too late! She couldn't retreat to the bathroom and change! And Truman was staring hard at the scanty black leather bra. It was sprinkled with silver metal studs and was designed so that it didn't even cover her nipples. The underwire pushed her breasts impossibly high, pressing them together, so flesh crested over dark leather like white frothy waves. She felt as if she was spilling out, solely for his gaze, the cups' black scalloped edges masterfully doing what they were designed to—framing aroused, reddened buds.

"I don't know why I wore it," she managed. The bra had been here for days, but tonight, out of curiosity, she'd slipped it on, just to see how it felt to wear something so naughty. Then realizing she was running late, she'd thrown on her T-shirt, and since the bra wasn't noticeable beneath it, she'd left it on.

Now her mind raced for excuses, and she pondered the even naughtier design of the matching panties. Somehow, she needed to remove the panties before Truman saw them! His burning gaze was making her feel too bare—not just physically, but emotionally. One glance at the bra, and he'd realize how much she'd been fantasizing...

With his eyes still caressing her breasts, she could barely talk. She was mortified, and her flush mixed with a wave of aroused warmth that washed over her skin. Her belly fluttered, then turned to water. "I don't usually wear things like this," she quickly explained. "Like I said, when I was in those stores, I *had* to buy something to get clerks to talk. I *had* to," she repeated with emphasis. "I didn't have a choice. You see, I bought this little number to...to..."

"Make me very happy?" Truman suggested thickly.

The heartfelt ravenous gaze assured her he liked the bra. Even more, he wanted what was in it. But she had to get to the bathroom and change! she thought, crimson staining her cheeks as she thought of the panties.

Blowing out a slow breath, he said, "This is beautiful, Trudy. You're beautiful."

The way he looked at her certainly made her feel that way. So did glancing down, which revealed his arousal. Clearly, the man meant every compliment. But it was too late to move. He'd rested the backs of his fingers on her bare tummy, very near the waistband of her jeans. A tremor shook her flesh as he dragged all ten digits slowly upward. Ten separate touches feathered over her ribs. Tingles scattered, spraying over bare skin until her thighs were quivering in anticipation. *Please, please, please,* she thought, hoping he'd touch her breasts very soon.

He took forever. Waiting tips further constricted, and she almost whimpered aloud, her breath shallowing as his fingers stopped a maddening inch away from the leather. Swallowing to conceal another throaty sound, she fought not to squirm, hoping she looked as if she knew what she was doing. If Truman guessed how much she wanted this, he might realize she'd never slept with a man before....

When he touched her breasts, the room seemed darker, and her emotions spun with expectation. Everything reeled. He kept his eyes on her face as his thumbs simultaneously circled each nipple, drawing out the pleasure, making her want to beg to feel his mouth there. Explosively hot, searingly wet—his mouth, when it came, shocked her whole system. He gave her time to accustom herself. Just as the rocketing sensations leveled off, he came again, this time with the strong thrust of his tongue and liquid fire that sponged her breasts. Lightening-fast flickers to the buds made edgy heat burn in her belly until she was silently begging for release. The strap of the bra seemed too tight around her ribs. Everything he did stole her breath.

Urgently, she gripped Truman's thighs, pushing her hands another tantalizing inch upward on worn denim, forgetting her plan to excuse herself and take off the panties before he noticed them. *Forget it,* she told herself. The panties were a bridge she'd cross when they came to it. Somehow, she'd manage to take them off before he noticed the shameless design....

He groaned as her palms settled on his hips, her

thumbs bracketing him, only inches from the erection straining his fly.

"Lie back," he whispered, the words rough and impatient as he unsnapped her jeans.

Scalding fire pored over her as she thought of her brazen underwear. Thinking she'd better warn him, she whispered, "The panties..."

"I bet they're really nice," Truman offered, his breath catching, his eyes looking dazed as he lay beside her. Slowly, he dragged down her jeans zipper, then his body pressed nearer, his lean, runner's legs trailing down hers. Against her hip, she felt the staggering pressure of his arousal. He was so male, so hot. Should she tell him she was a virgin? Surely, he was assuming she'd done all this before.

But what if he stopped? No, she wasn't going to say a word! She was going to just go for it.

Her breath caught and her hips twitched reflexively as Truman edged between her legs, scooting his hands beneath her, the hot tip of his tongue lazily trailing from her breasts, over flaming, sensitized skin, down to her belly. He swirled his tongue around her navel more times than she could count, then sprinkled wet kisses an inch lower, concentrating them between her navel and the open fly of her jeans.

"Relax," he whispered, the encouraging tone so tender she wanted to cry. If only he knew how long she'd waited for this! And why? What had she feared? Her mind hazed as he kissed her. Why hadn't she said yes to this before? She'd been such an idiot! She was an adult. She could have been doing this every day of her life...

Losing herself to bliss, she let him slip her jeans

down, pushing denim over her hips and thighs. Glancing down, she felt her heart miss a beat when she noticed the mound pushing against his zipper. Her fingers burned to reach for him. She desperately wanted to touch that fabric—and everything inside. She couldn't rip her eyes away. He looked so powerful there. So ready. She held back another cry.

"More than nice," he uttered on a growl, as he took in the panties. They were low cut. Black. Studded. But so far, he hadn't noticed the naughty slit in them. Curling his hands around her knees, he tenderly stroked the backs, then glided his touch upward, its warmth pure heaven on her skin. Gently, insistently, he urged her to part her legs farther for him, but she struggled to keep them together as another scalding wave crested inside her. Realizing he was going to notice the slit in the panties eventually, damp tingles cascaded over her skin. She wanted to part for him, she admitted nervously, she really did. But then he'd see...

He'd see...

A breathless whisper met her ears. "You feel like silk, Trudy. So soft. I can't believe it."

Muscular biceps banked her thighs. Pecs as smooth as marble grazed the tops of her legs. His breath was on her belly, his chin only inches from the still-closed slit in the triangle of black leather when he huskily added, "Don't fight me, Trudy."

She couldn't if she wanted to. "I won't. I'm not."

"Yes, you are."

Truman's chin lowered a frustrating fraction, and his gaze was still hot on hers when he nuzzled her through the leather. His face was beautiful, she thought, mindlessly taking in the slanted, sensual, whiskey-colored eyes, and the astonishing breadth of the broad shoulders spanning her legs. His hair was long enough that feather-like wisps swept her bare skin.

Suddenly melting like butter, she opened—quickly, involuntarily—and he gasped when he realized the panties were no more functional than the bra. His breath came hard. "You have no idea what you're doing to me," he whispered, jerking his head to get the hair out of his eyes and pressing his thumb to the leather, widening the slit so he could see her. "Oh, Trudy," he said simply.

Her heart was pounding. "You like them?"

"More than like them." He stroked her. "You're... perfect."

A pant gave way to a guttural groan as he lowered his chin, pressing his face to her, brushing her with his lips as he inhaled deeply to take her musk. No longer able to contain the bursting cries of pleasure, Trudy bit her lower lip, hoping she wouldn't buck against him like a fool.

His hand found her mouth. His thumb forced apart her lips. On a hot pant, he demanded, "Let me hear you, Trudy."

An uncontrolled whimper rent the air. And, oh, the pleasure! The silk heat of his mouth drenched her then, his tongue pushing into the leather rip, his hands tucking beneath her and lifting her shamelessly for the kiss. She began twisting, sobbing, "Stop, stop..."

He stopped.

"No," she gasped. She hadn't meant that, not really. "Please. I mean, please..."

He did her bidding each time. Her whole body flaming, she thought he'd never be done with her. She was going mad. Completely out of her mind as the magic of that mouth pooled where she ached, soaking her, pouring fire in her blood. Every fiber of her craved more when, from what seemed a million miles away, she heard the slow whir of a motor. "No!" she gasped. Okay, she could admit it. She was going to try that, but not with him, not with a man....

Wet fire coated her as he stroked her thighs, willing her to trust him as the hard vibrating tip hovered where she was so open. Slowly, he eased the device inside. His mouth found her once more. Even as his tongue was on her, he slowly, gently, moved the vibrator inside her. Her hands clawed the mattress, her nails raked down the sheet.

The room vanished. Nothing existed. Just this pleasure, and the man giving it. Orgasm after orgasm burst through her, the endless pulling sensations making the world fade to black. She might have fainted. She wasn't sure. Wild hands caressed his shoulders, fingers dug into the ridges of his back, then thrust upward, tangling and fisting in his hair. When silence returned, he'd left her weak, defenseless, thoroughly invaded. She'd never known such pleasure existed.

And then, in a voice silken with seduction, the fool man had the nerve to whisper, "I think you're about ready now, Trudy."

She felt otherworldly, her body no longer something that belonged to her. But no...she belonged to him now. To Truman Steele. She was his, all his. She'd never felt anything like this. He started to remove the panties and bra, but she said, "Hurry."

He shook his head. "I want you naked."

She was naked enough. "Later," she whispered urgently. "Please! Now!"

His whiskey-colored eyes were dazed with lust, and he wasn't about to waste time arguing. Inhaling through clenched teeth, he stripped off his jeans. Freed, he was hard and gorgeous. And when he came to her, his turgid flesh parting the leather and seeking her, she accepted him fully, as part of herself.

She'd never felt so close to anyone, never felt anything so powerful as when he thrust inside, filling her. "You're so tight," he whispered hoarsely. "I thought only virgins were this tight."

She couldn't answer. She was climbing, stretching for another peak, taking all of him, pulling him closer with each thrusting embrace, so they were heart to heart when he went over the edge.

"Really," he whispered later, when their breath had evened and he was contenting himself with cradling a hand around the head curled on his chest and burying kisses in her hair. "You felt like a virgin, Trudy Busey."

Before, she hadn't wanted him to know. Now everything was different. Truman Steele had become a part of her. Instead of feeling exposed, she felt completely accepted, so she said, "A few minutes ago, I was one, Truman."

"WHAT DID YOU SAY?" Truman's heart, which had almost stilled, now missed a beat. He'd just removed her underwear, and now he rolled to his side, tucking her into the crook of his arm. He'd never felt anything like this woman. Touching her electrified him. Her taste sent his senses reeling. But more than that, her responsiveness had stolen his heart. He'd been completely blown away. She was the most passionate woman he'd ever met. Now his hand curled, the tips of his fingers tightening on her head before he began smoothing her hair.

"I should have told you, Truman," she whispered, sounding dreamy and contrite. "I'm sorry I didn't, really I am."

Call it a cop's suspicious mind, but Trudy simply couldn't be telling him the truth. But no. When she glanced up at him, those beautiful, clear blue eyes were without guile. His barely audible words were incredulous. "You've never slept with anybody, Trudy?"

He thought the slow, self-satisfied grin tugging her lips was heart-stopping, and when she lowered her head to his chest once more, he felt the curve of the smile on his bare skin. She whispered, "Does heavy petting count?"

He shook his head. "No. Are you really telling me that before tonight, you'd never..."

"Now I have."

With that, she traced a heart on his chest and drew an arrow through it.

He loved that she did that. She was amazing. She meshed with him on an intellectual level, and in bed, she was insatiable. Now, she was cuddlesome as a kitten. His mind raced over what they'd done, and he couldn't think of what to say first. Right now, he couldn't believe Trudy Busey even existed. He'd assumed she'd avoided deep relationships, but it never occurred to him that she didn't have an active sex life. She was so different from every other woman he'd ever met, so special...

Which was why, if he'd known she'd never slept

with anyone, he would have loved her the proper way first. His heart tugged as he stroked her cheek. "Why didn't you tell me?"

"I was afraid you'd stop," she said pragmatically.

"Once we got going," he assured, "the end of the world couldn't have stopped me."

"Me, neither."

His throat tightened against the questions he wanted to ask. Had she chosen him simply because she wanted sex? Or had the temptation of the toys been more than she could stand? His heart lurched, and he had to admit he was hoping for only one answer: that she'd done it because she liked him. He was hoping she'd only held back before tonight due to her assumptions about his depravity. Because of that, it took courage to say it. "Why me, Trudy?"

She laughed like an excited kid, the sound so sweetly irresistible that he couldn't help but smile in return, his eyes warming as he took in the play of shadows on the silky pale strands of her hair. "I really don't know," she admitted on a deep sigh, looking terribly pleased with herself.

He shot her a dubious glance. "You made a life-altering decision and you don't know why? You're too smart for that, Trudy. You don't act without thinking."

"Are you grilling me, Steele?" she teased, squinting playfully as she fished around her ankles, pulling up a sheet to cover their chests. "If so, I warn you, I'm a force to be reckoned with."

"So I've discovered."

"Maybe you should call for backup."

"No way. I want you all to myself. I'm not sharing."

She didn't look convinced. "You promise you're not

going to put me on the other side of a two-way mirror and interrogate me?"

"No. I've found other ways to make you talk."

She laughed. "You have, indeed."

He kissed her lightly, affection that surprised him swelling his heart and spreading warmth through his limbs. When he nestled back, enjoying the feel of her in his arms, she shrugged again. "I guess, there's a spark between us. Right, Truman?"

He surveyed her. "You have to ask?"

She nodded slowly. "It's pretty strong for me."

"Yeah," he couldn't help but tease, "now that you realize I'm not a sex pervert."

Tilting her head, she considered. "After what just happened, the jury's still out on that." Before he could fire back a quip, she added, "What about you?" He could see her throat working as she swallowed, the vulnerability behind her tough facade almost painfully evident. "Any attraction on your part?"

How could she doubt it? He thought a moment, then admitted, "The strongest I've ever felt, Trudy."

"Now you're getting too serious."

She had no idea. "Do you want to get married?" Feeling her tense against him, he drew her even closer. "Don't push me away," he murmured, knowing she'd avoided relationships and that she'd probably try.

"I can't promise I won't," she said honestly. "Proposing before we know each other is something I find kind of spooky."

He sighed, once more unable to believe he'd loved her through a bra and panties. "If I'd known you'd never..."

"You would have what?" she challenged lightly, relaxing again against his side, threading her fingers absently in his sparse silken gold chest hair. "Done everything differently?"

"I confess." He smiled. "I would at least have undressed you."

Resting her chin comfortably on his chest, she eyed him. "You don't like what happened?"

Uttering a gasp of protest, he said, "I love what happened." In fact, he was ready to make it happen again.

"But you'd trade that for..." She paused, tracing more maddening designs on his bare skin, making him aware of the heat from her body, the soft crush of her breasts. "What?" she continued. "Dinner? Candy? Flowers? A movie?"

"You've got a point. Still, I would have..." He shrugged, trying to think. "I don't know. Made it special."

She laughed outright, the abandonment of her joy making her seem like a whole other person than the one he'd met at the precinct. And yet he knew she was the same, that something very important had happened tonight. Trudy Busey rarely let down her guard, but she'd let him in. Just a little. She'd made herself vulnerable, and it felt special, like a gift. Already, he wanted more. Trudy was the sort of woman who'd only choose a man once. Truman wanted to be that man.

"Truman," she murmured, the crazy circles she was drawing on his skin arousing him in a way that would soon demand satisfaction. "I think my outfit qualified as special."

He chuckled. "That's hard to argue with."

She poked him in the ribs. "Then quit arguing."

"Okay," he whispered, and for a moment, they fell silent, staring through the gauze of the curtain at the green neon burger hanging above Billy's Burgers. Outside, far below in the street, a car was holding up traffic, and people laid on their horns. "I think that's what I always hate the most," she said after the horns fell silent. "I mean about dating."

He sighed, still amazed by the uncanny physical perfection they'd achieved, and by how their breaths were falling in synch. "What?"

"All the candy and flowers."

He frowned. "Most women love that stuff."

She arched a brow. "Gee thanks. Do I look like most women?"

"No. Another excellent point goes to Trudy Busey," he conceded.

Satisfied, she settled on his chest again. "Every time men treat me like a lady, I just..."

"Freeze up because you feel like everything's too formal?"

She nodded. "I want to be treated with respect, of course, but I'm not made of glass."

Between the lines, he'd begun to wonder how much respect she'd gotten at home. On their ride-along, she'd talked about her family. They sounded nice, but overprotective, and she was the only girl. He figured her mother had died, but she'd never said. "I respect you, Trudy."

She smirked. "I don't mean in the morning."

But she did. "I know what you mean," he countered. "And I respect you," he repeated. "As a professional. *And* in the morning." When she stilled in his arms, he knew she was considering whether to trust him, and he added, "You're smart. Driven. I know they don't give you the stories you want at the *News*, but you'll hang in there, and eventually they'll have to."

Her voice caught with hope. "How do you know that?"

"Because you're a winner. You've got what it takes."

If he'd ever said a right thing in his life, it was at that moment. Her blue eyes shined. "You really think so?"

"I've met a lot of reporters. You're good. You're just a new kid on the block. You're a woman, too. That doesn't help. And you're pretty as hell."

She stared at him for long moments. "Want to team up?" she finally asked. "You solve the Glass Slipper case?"

"And you get the scoop?" he guessed. It was everything he'd hoped for. He'd imagined quickly hashing out the ride-along article with some reporter, but instead of a Dan Rather type, he'd gotten Trudy. Her suggestion shouldn't have hurt, since in another circumstance he would have welcomed it, but his teasing tone didn't hide his doubts when he probed. "Using me for a story, huh?"

"Trust doesn't come easy," she surmised. "Because you're a cop? Or because of something personal?"

Darker emotion surfaced as he thought of Sue. Ten years ago, he'd been too young and macho to give a woman her personal space. He couldn't have been with a woman as career-oriented and ambitious as Trudy. "It's been a long time since I've wanted to get close to anybody," he admitted, brushing back her hair with his fingertips and feeling a thrill at the touch. "I almost got married when I was younger, right out of the academy, but I...I didn't. Her name was Sue."

"What happened?"

"Long story," he said. "Too heavy for tonight."

"Talk," she warned, her reporter's instincts kicking into high gear. "Or you're out on the street, Steele."

"You'd throw me out like this?"

She shrugged. "Maybe I'd toss you your underwear."

His eyes roved over her, the mock threat lightening the mood, putting him off-guard. Around her, interview subjects would always say more than they meant to. "You make it easy."

"What?"

"Talking."

"It's my job."

Even if it wasn't, he'd feel compelled to share himself with her. He snuggled closer. "We got pregnant. I figured we'd get married someday, but when that happened, I proposed." He shrugged, unable to verbalize the feelings. They were too dark. He'd felt as if his heart had been ripped out of his chest. Something inside him had been irreparably crushed. "She backed out when she miscarried. She wasn't very far along, just two months." Just long enough for him to experience all the joys of expectant fatherhood.

Her voice was the gentlest he'd ever heard. "You lost the baby?"

"It was a long time ago." Light years. Sue's face, once so sharp in his mind, was only a blur now. "After that," he forced himself to continue, "I dated more casually." He brushed a kiss to Trudy's forehead. "Really," he said again, "it's too heavy a topic for the night we've begun."

"Begun?" She laughed softly. "It's two in the morning, Truman. The night's about over."

"Fortunately, I've got a drive-along partner who won't mind if I'm groggy tomorrow."

"There might be other nights, Truman," she ventured.

"There's another night less than twenty-four hours from now," he assured. The toys no longer piquing his interest, he started imagining the next time with Trudy. He wanted her. All of her. Nothing but her. "Tomorrow night," he whispered, "it's just you and me. No toys, Trudy."

"Tonight," she corrected in a whisper. "Since it's two o'clock in the morning, it's already tomorrow."

Holding her closer, he urged her to shut her eyes and sleep in his embrace, whispering, "Then you'd better get some sleep, Trudy." He smiled. "Because tonight, you're going to need it."

5

THREE DAYS LATER, as he stepped from the shower in his one-bedroom apartment on Waverly Place overlooking Washington Square Park, Truman decided he was getting too old for these late nights. He'd refrained from taking fresh uniforms to Trudy's because he didn't want to scare her by keeping clothes there too soon, but that meant he had to rush home every day to change.

This morning he'd rather have showered together and shared breakfast. Maybe at that Southern-style eatery on Grand Street. They served the works—biscuits and gravy, fried potatoes and grits. His stomach growling, Truman grabbed a towel from the rack, drying himself as he headed for the bedroom. He was dressing when the cell phone rang. Switching it on, he said, "Morning."

There were no preliminaries. "Have you talked to Pop?"

"Rex," he said, suppressing disappointment when it wasn't Trudy. He'd left her apartment an hour ago, but he already missed her and he couldn't wait to pick her up in the patrol car again. As much as he wanted to return to his regular route, Trudy was providing an adrenaline rush that couldn't match that of the city streets. Besides, he'd be back on patrol soon enough. Meantime, he and Trudy were cruising the Upper

West Side today with scheduled public-relations stops at Uptown precincts. The mayor was getting flak for closing mental health facilities, so pressure was on Trudy to beef up the story. A *News* photographer was meeting them later. Tucking the phone under his chin, Truman shrugged into a uniform shirt and stared toward the stone arch marking the entrance to the park.

Usually, his trained eyes noticed litter, or pickpockets opening trench coats to expose stolen watches they wanted to hawk, or lowlifes who took the subway into Manhattan hoping to con unsuspecting tourists. Today, however, he saw only jays and sparrows flitting through the trees and couples walking dogs or sitting on benches, happily kissing and holding hands while sharing coffee and croissants. Great sex could definitely change a man's perspective.

"You there, Truman? Did you go back to sleep?"

"I'm awake." His attention returned to the call. "Good morning to you, too. And no. I haven't talked to Pop for—" He paused to think. "Oh, I don't know, Rex. A week or so."

"Ma's worried. She says he's working too many late nights."

Rummaging in a drawer for socks that matched, Truman said, "Pop always works late."

"Not so much now that he's managing money."

Truman bit back a laugh. Their father had started out as a beat cop in Hell's Kitchen, but he'd climbed the ladder and was poised to retire from the force as an administrator, overseeing budgetary concerns and managing police-related monetary accounts. "He's not even on the street anymore. He's pushing paper, Rex. He's fine."

Rex chuckled. "You're probably right, but I wouldn't let him hear you say that. Anyway, Ma wants us to check up on him. Maybe go downtown and have lunch, since lately, he's been too busy to come home during the day."

"What?" scoffed Truman. "You make it sound like Ma thinks he's having an affair or something."

Rex grunted in protest since their father was such a straight arrow. "She knows he'd never do that. She's just worried, says he's not his usual self. All she wants is a second opinion."

Truman thought of Trudy. "Sure, but I'm still doing that drive-along thing. You know, with..." he paused, then decided to play it safe for the moment "...the reporter from the *News*."

"No rush. Pop's busy till the end of next week. Says if we wait until then to come down to Police Plaza, we can head over to Wall Street and have ribs at that place near the Stock Exchange. Food's on him."

"Hot damn. I love that joint. Should I call Sully?"

"I'll do it. But speaking of late nights, where have you been? Sully says he's tried to call you for days. All he gets is your machine. Even at four in the morning. Whoever she is, it must be serious, little brother."

Truman smiled, lifting his gun belt from around the back of a chair. "Do I seem like a guy who kisses and tells?"

"No, but I was hoping for vicarious thrills."

"Don't tell me you're having no luck finding a wife? I just assumed you and Sully were as busy as me."

Rex made another low throaty sound of amusement. "Doubtful. Sully's too busy going head to head with that hellcat from Internal Affairs. What's her name?"

Before Truman could respond, Rex continued, "Judith Hunt. That's it. He swears she's trying to arrest every decent cop in his precinct. By the end of the day, he says the last thing he wants to see is a woman. In fact, he says next time he sweeps Little Italy and arrests the mob, he's going to be tempted to hang on to one of their hit men."

Truman hooted. "She must really be under his skin."

"You can't blame him," Rex said, speaking more seriously. "Sully's honest as the day is long. No doubt, at least one guy in his precinct's on the take, but if so, it's penny-ante. Judith Hunt's sniffing around, barking up the wrong tree."

Truman considered, knowing Rex wasn't condoning anything illegal. New York was the most expensive city in the country, and when men with wives and kids to support took money to look the other way, the Steeles tried to view them with pity, not moralistic superiority. "A cop-hating cop," sighed Truman. "And even Sully admits she's easy on the eyes. She must be hot."

"She is. I've met her. Anyway, what about you?"

"Well," admitted Truman, "I met somebody."

"Your future bride?" Rex said incredulously. "You're joking, right? You're not taking this whole thing with Ma and the Galapagos Islands to heart, are you?"

"Do you want to give fifteen million dollars to a bunch of turtles?" countered Truman.

"Ma's not really going to give the money away. You know that. She's just trying to pressure us into meeting some new women." There was a long silence during which both men contemplated the huge win. Over the past few days, Truman had found himself imagining buying a brownstone like his parents'. He figured he could rent the upstairs floors, since such buildings were so expensive to maintain. Maybe he'd marry Trudy, start a family...

Sucking in a quick breath, he abruptly thrust his feet into shoes and leaned, lacing them. Was he ready to give his heart again? To risk being hurt? Could he marry Trudy, just to get his hands on the money—and not tell her? He was glad when Rex grunted. "Did you tell this person you're going to marry her?"

"Yeah. But she didn't believe me."

"Who is she?" Before Truman could answer, Rex added, "And what did you do? Assault her with roses and chocolates?"

Truman warmed, recalling their first night together. "She hates candy and flowers."

"My kind of girl. Does she have any sisters?"

"Sorry, only brothers. And whether you like it or not, she's not your type. You're a romantic, Rex. This one's ambitious."

"Blond, brunette or redhead?"

"I take back everything I just said about your poetic soul. Don't you know it's the inside that counts?" After a beat Truman added, "Blond."

"Ten to one, her name's Candy."

"Wrong," returned Truman. "But given the notes Candy's putting under my windshield wipers, she's still available. If you want her number, I've got it in triplicates."

"Maybe later, little brother. Meantime, hang on to it for me. And I'll believe you're serious about this other woman when you bring her home for lunch. And I don't mean next week with Pop. Bring her to the house. Introduce her to Ma."

Truman considered. "How's tomorrow sound?"

Right before Rex replaced the receiver, he laughed. "This should be interesting."

"YOUR HOME'S LOVELY," Trudy remarked to Sheila, glancing around the leafy courtyard and enjoying a light summer breeze that was blowing fine strands of hair against her cheeks.

"Thank you," said the other woman.

For a moment, they admired the view in silence. Sully and Rex had just left, and now Truman scooted closer, draping an arm along the back of Trudy's chair. Comforting heat seeped through his uniform, warming her side, while under the table, the hand cupping her thigh climbed an inch higher. Usually, she would have been embarrassed to exhibit a physical relationship, but the Steeles had barely noticed.

Or rather, they took such things in stride. They were a physical bunch. Sheila hugged and kissed. Sully, Rex and Truman clapped shoulders and backs. All very unlike the Busey family—very unlike any people Trudy had ever met, she corrected with a smile—but strangely she hadn't felt left out. The Steele men were close, but they didn't exclude women. Truman had stayed near her during the visit—rubbing a shoulder or patting a hand—offering small, caring gestures to assure her she belonged.

"From the sidewalks," Trudy continued, trying to ignore the maddening circles Truman began tracing on her thigh, "you'd never guess places this green exist in the city." Squinting, she leaned forward, resting her elbows on the glass-topped table where Sheila had served lunch. "You know," she added, the idea sparking, "Human interest stories don't intrigue me as much as others, but I'd love to do a piece about this place. I think Dimi—he's my editor—would go for it."

Sheila smiled, delighted. "A story...?" she murmured, her eyes taking in the courtyard as if seeing it for the first time, looking almost wistful as her attention strayed past ferns and flowers to things left behind as her sons grew—a stone sandbox, a tire swing, the childhood handprints pressed into the patio's cement and the painted lines on a tree marking their comparative heights. "A story?" she repeated. "About my garden?"

Truman caught Trudy's eye and merely shook his head. He murmured, "Doesn't your mind ever quit, Busey? This is lunch, not work."

Under the table, she slid her hand over the back of his, threading her fingers between his. "Steele," she countered playfully, "do you have something against women with creative, active brains?"

Awareness came into his eyes. "Not since I met you."

"Good answer." Shooting him a pointed look, she turned her attention to his mother once more. "I don't know," she began. "In this garden, there's something so..."

"Romantic?" suggested Sheila, eyeing Trudy and her son.

"Yes," returned Trudy enthusiastically. "That's exactly the right word. Romantic. There's so much undiscovered greenery in the city. Strange," she added. "Lately, I've been noticing it more and more."

"Oh, have you?" asked Sheila, still glancing between Trudy and her son and looking amused.

"Yes," returned Trudy, missing the irony. "So many quiet getaways. Rooftop gardens. Actually," she paused, tilting her head and gazing into the middle distance. "We could photograph a number of gardens. It would make a terrific coffee-table book."

Eyes very like Truman's sparkled, and Sheila brushed back flyaway strands of hair that had fallen from her practical gray bun. "Through C.L.A.S.P., I met an editor from Random House who works on coffee-table books. Maybe she'd be interested. We could call it *Manhattan Getaways,* or maybe *Romancing New York.*"

"There's a photographer at the *News* who shoots landscapes in his spare time," Trudy said, picking up the thread and envisioning a big, beautiful hardcover with the kind of pictures that would inspire readers' dreams. "I'll talk to him later today." Trudy's eyes narrowed. "You mentioned C.L.A.S.P. Isn't that the City and Local Activists for Street People?"

Sheila nodded. "I've been involved for a while."

Truman groaned. "Involved? Don't let her fool you, Trudy. Ma's a charter member. And don't get her started on local politics," he warned. "If you think lunch was good, you should hear her roast our mayor."

Trudy chuckled, squeezing his hand, then sobered. "I've spent a lot of time down at Bryant Park recently," she admitted. "Some of the people I've interviewed are in real trouble."

"Whenever the mayor closes hospitals, it's bad,"

Truman said. "Our precinct's doing what it can. Lots of guys have brought in clothing donations."

As Truman picked up the conversation, Trudy tamped down the memories of following him through the park...and of what happened afterward. Ever since, he'd been courting her, and with that, came excitement, passion and ecstasy, things she'd never allowed herself to feel before now. Everything around her suddenly seemed bursting and fresh, as sunny and bright as the garden where they were seated, as new as the green buds pushing through the bark of the trees.

New and fresh. Yes, that's how she felt inside. But maybe she was becoming too open to her feelings, she thought now. Because she felt scared, too. Sometimes, the awakening almost hurt. Sure, she'd said she didn't like candy and flowers. But she did. And Truman kept bringing them, licking chocolate from her bare skin and tearing off rose petals until they covered her, making everything smell like the world after a spring rain.

As it turned out, Truman's apartment was more spacious, but hers came to belong to them. With two people there, it should have felt cramped. Instead, it felt like a love nest. Or den of iniquity, she thought, warmth spreading through her limbs. Night after night, they fled there, discovering new pleasures, drowning in them.

In the morning, after he was gone, it would hit her. The fear would come unexpectedly, in a dark wave. Worry would creep in. Firmly, she'd tell herself the anxiety belonged to her past. She feared she'd become like her mother if she gave herself to Truman. Maybe, like her mother, she wasn't capable of caring about both a career and a man. She'd become dependant. Reliant. Weak. She'd never succeed.

And then, like her mother, maybe she'd run away from everything she was supposed to love.

"Yes?" Trudy suddenly said, realizing Truman and Sheila had fallen silent. She pressed a hand to her heart, her cheeks coloring. "I guess I..."

"Spaced out?" Sheila provided with a carefree laugh. "This garden will do it. Coming here is like stepping out of time."

"It's beautiful," Trudy agreed, glancing around. When her eyes settled on the tree where the Steele boys had marked their heights, she mulled over her impressions of the men she'd met today. Sully had been calm and collected. Rex, scruffy and dreamy. And Truman...

Her heart softened. He tried so hard around his brothers, maybe too hard. Even now, he was fighting not to be the youngest, to make his mark with the men in his family. Because it was her own struggle, Trudy understood it deeply, and she'd never been so moved by him as when she'd watched him today, interacting with Sully and Rex.

Truman squeezed her knee. "If the garden's made you step out of time," he teased, "I hope you're going all the way back to Eden."

Trudy frowned. "As in the garden of?"

Truman grinned. "I like the outfits."

"They were doing okay until she ate that apple," Trudy conceded dryly.

"That's why I brought you here for lunch," he shot back. "If I keep you well fed, maybe you won't be tempted."

She pinched him playfully, and his mother laughed,

taking the humor in stride. Sobering, Trudy said honestly, "I'm glad I met your brothers." Her gaze took in Sheila, adding, "Sons." She'd liked meeting Sheila, too. The other woman, clearly not easily threatened, had made her feel welcome and accepted.

"I'm only sorry my husband couldn't join us," Sheila said, shaking her head and looking worried.

Trudy's reporterly instincts kicked in. Her gaze deepened with concern. "Me, too. When we highlight Truman in the *New York News* article, I'll be mentioning that he comes from a family of officers. It would be nice to meet your husband."

"Ma's worried," Truman explained. "Pop's working too much."

Trudy shrugged. "Ambition's something I understand." And yet there could be so much more, she thought, becoming conscious of Truman's hand on her knee again. The feeling was confusing, though. She fought the urge to edge away. Her job demanded so much time. Realistically, how much could she give up?

They hadn't yet spent a night apart, and she wasn't sure of her boundaries yet. Was this too much, too fast? Should she trust it? Was it sex or something more? Did she really want something more? Her throat tightened. Yes. She wanted the security love brought. Heat swirled in her belly as she thought of how they'd experimented with each item she'd bought near Bryant Park. She'd never suspected how quickly lovemaking could make her feel reliant on a man. She felt uncertain, and wished she had an older woman like Sheila with whom she could talk.

"This time," Truman guessed, "you're thinking about me."

And how. Trudy smiled. "You might be right."

"So you were in Bryant Park?" Sheila prompted.

Trudy nodded, shaking her head to clear it. "I was shooting pictures and interviewing people, hoping to pitch a longer, in-depth story to the *News*. Actually, if you don't mind, I'd love to stop by the new women's shelter C.L.A.S.P. is opening in the meat-packing district, maybe talk to some people."

"Come anytime, but I'm only there on weekdays. I try to spend weekends at home."

"I'll come when you're there," said Trudy warmly, wanting to get to know Sheila further. "I want to write the kind of story that will make people pay attention."

"What other stories are you working on?"

Because Sheila was genuinely interested, Trudy elaborated more than she usually would. "I get all kinds of assignments. Right now, I'm spending most of the day with Truman. While I feel pressured to do a story that's strictly public relations, I'm searching for a special angle, something truthful, but that still shows New York in its best light."

Truman laughed. "That's not what you said a week ago."

He was thinking of their first meeting. She smiled again. "Let's just say my mood's improved."

"I hope I've had something to do with that."

Of course he had. Her eyes glinted with humor. "Maybe." Turning to Sheila, she continued, "I've got other interests you share." Earlier, she'd realized Sheila had a passion for the Galapagos Islands. "The environment, for instance. The original reporter got sick, so I'm doing a follow-up piece on the Galapagos oil spill."

"You're a bundle of energy," said Sheila on a pleased sigh.

"Oh," added Trudy, excitement about her work propelling her. "And there's the lottery story."

Sheila leaned forward. "Lottery?"

Trudy nodded, registering a glance that passed between mother and son. It was faint, just a tremor of awareness grew inside her, but she could swear Sheila knew...*something*. "Someone just won one of the biggest jackpots in New York history," Trudy explained. "Fifteen million dollars. It's a fortune. But the person has asked not to be identified."

"I seem to recall something about that," murmured Sheila.

Something unreadable crossed Truman's features.

"We ran a lot of man-in-the-street interviews," Trudy continued. "Now, people are demanding to know the outcome. It never occurred to us that the winner wouldn't want newspaper coverage."

"Any idea why the person isn't talking?" asked Sheila.

Trudy pretended she didn't notice the quelling glance Truman sent his mother. What was going on here? She wondered. "Maybe the person's famous," she suggested blandly. "That's the most popular theory at the *News*. If they're already rich and keep the money, they'll be attacked. People will say they should donate it to a charity."

"Or maybe they're making a silent contribution?" suggested Sheila. "Charitable deeds are more noble if not advertised."

"Could be," agreed Trudy.

Sheila suddenly laughed, leaned and pinched her

son's arm. "Or maybe some poor, hopeless mother like me has got a bunch of grown bachelors for sons," she teased. "And when she won, she said she wouldn't split the money between them until they got married."

The idea was so ludicrous that Trudy laughed. The feeling that the Steeles were hiding something dissipated. No, there was nothing here. Trudy got false glimmers of intuition all the time. It was the downside to having a suspicious reporter's mind. "Your mother's dangerous," Trudy warned.

"Oh," returned Truman dryly. "You have no idea."

Trudy's laugh tempered to a chuckle. "Well, whoever won, I'd love to find out why they're not announcing it." She added, "It would be the next best thing to walking in their shoes."

"Some shoes," agreed Truman.

Trudy nodded her agreement. "Even swankier than the ones stolen by our Prince Charming."

"You're ambitious, dedicated and perceptive," said Sheila, her eyes twinkling. "Who knows, Trudy? Maybe you'll eventually wind up breaking that lottery story."

6

TRUMAN SHIFTED HIS weight on a chaise longue later that night, gliding a hand down Trudy's back and easing his thighs farther apart, guiding her so she wedged between them. Their legs twined, the arches of her bare feet curling against his calves and warming themselves in the folds of his blue jeans. "Sorry, I had to move," he murmured as her arms wrapped around his waist. She pressed her cheek to his chest. She was braless and under the silk dress she'd changed into after work, he could feel the rise of her breasts, and the change in texture where her nipples relaxed.

"This chair's small for us both," she conceded.

"Parts of me were falling asleep."

"The parts that aren't waking up, anyway." When she stared at him, candle flames caught in her irises, turning her blue eyes violet in the darkness. Her dress, too, was more violet than blue. Short-sleeved and silk, it was loose and long, rippling to her ankles. From the feel of it, she wasn't wearing a stitch beneath.

His voice dropped a notch. "We can go inside, Tru." *To bed.*

"In a minute, Tru," she returned, using the interchangeable pet name they'd picked for each other as she stared at the skyline. Through a break in the buildings shooting up all around them, he could see the top spire of the Empire State Building, brilliantly lit in pink to usher in summer.

"It's nice up here," he murmured, feeling torn since he wanted to be here and in bed. "I didn't know you had a roof garden," he added, regretting there was still so much he didn't know about Trudy. His gaze drifted to where she lay between his legs, and he smiled lazily. "You were holding out on me."

"Well, it's not *really* a roof garden," she defended.

"It won't make it into the book, huh?"

"Doubtful." Looking pleased that she'd interested the *News* photographer in the possible coffee-table book, she surveyed the lawn chairs she'd grouped in a conversational circle, then the few potted plants and an overturned cardboard box covered with a lace tablecloth. Long yellow flames of ten or so mismatched candles flickered over the remainder of dinner—Indian take-out cartons, a bowl of grapes and a half-finished bottle of Merlot. "I wasn't holding out on you," she promised. "Being at your mother's the other day reminded me I hadn't come up here since last summer."

Truman took in some spray-painted graffiti as he lifted fine strands of hair that looked straw yellow in the light and pressed a kiss to them. "Someone else has."

"Just neighborhood kids. And graffiti is art," Trudy schooled. "It's got a certain charm. This wouldn't be New York without it. Besides," she joked, "I'm a little broke. I couldn't afford a Picasso."

It was tempting to inform her that, if she married him, she could. A small etching anyway, Truman imagined, taking into account the exorbitant price of artwork. At that moment, five million dollars didn't seem like nearly so much money. Taxes would take half. Whatever was left after Uncle Sam would barely buy a brownstone in the city.

Before the lottery win, Truman hadn't realized how large a part finances played in his unwillingness to settle down. His mother had come from money, without which the Steeles never could have afforded their family home and even so, the upstairs floors were rented. Truman sighed. Anywhere else in the country, a cop's salary would be ample, but as his father always said, you could run a mile-long tab in New York just by breathing. It was why so many New York cops went on the take.

Using his free hand, he lifted a goblet and took a deep, heady draught of wine. Stroking Trudy's hair, he briefly shut his eyes, feeling warmth sliding into his body. He savored the liquid heat that burned down his throat, licked through his belly, then spread over his groin. "Graffiti as art?" he murmured. "You have strange taste."

"Only in men," she assured.

"You haven't had enough men to know if I'm strange."

"I shouldn't have told you I was a virgin," she complained.

"Ancient history," he reminded.

"We have put a lot of distance between then and now."

He nodded agreement. "Do me a favor and keep that roof-door locked. I don't want kids coming up the fire escape and getting inside your building. They could break into your apartment."

"Aren't you ever off-duty?"

His pointed glance was meant to indicate he was wearing street clothes, jeans and a white, button-down shirt. "These look like civilian clothes to me."

She chuckled again, all wide-eyed innocence. "My, my," she murmured, pressing harder against him. "That's not a gun?"

"No, that's definitely something else." His lips twitched with humor. "My interest in you is strictly personal."

"The weapon's your own?"

"Careful," he warned. "It's loaded."

She shot him a look of mock disdain. "For your information, I don't go looking for trouble." She poked him in the ribs. "Of course, sometimes trouble finds me."

"You're calling me trouble?"

"Take it however you wish," she returned lightly.

A hand tightened on her back, hauling her closer as he took another sip of wine. This time, he felt the alcohol hit the back of his neck. She pulled his head down for a slow, languorous kiss, one full and wet with desire and wine. Angling his lips across hers, he deepened the onslaught, the pressure firmer as he took more of her mouth, her taste.

Moments later, as he drew away, she licked at the traces of lingering taste and said, "I found somebody at the lottery office who might talk to me. An assistant named Gracie Dale. She glimpsed the lottery check when it was cut, so if she chooses, she can identify the recipient." She'd told him since no one else was turning up leads, she'd gotten Dimi's permission to try.

"Really?" Truman struggled to keep his voice nonchalant. "Wouldn't she lose her job?"

"If she got caught telling me."

While Truman's mother loved playing inside jokes, her behavior during lunch had been unconscionable. First she'd threatened to withhold the lottery money if the women her sons were interested in suspected it existed, and then she'd openly encouraged Trudy to pursue the story. Since the lottery was the last thing he wanted to talk about, Truman urged Trudy to further relax against him. As close as she was, she still seemed too far away. Setting aside the glass, he used both arms to pull her into an embrace. Sighing, he splayed his fingers to better curve them over her buttocks, palming the flesh until he was rewarded by the arch of her hips. For a blessed minute, she connected with him, and he bit back a gasp at the joining, his body harder, his mind drifting.

"Tomorrow," she suddenly said, becoming strangely still. "I'd better stay in my office. I want to work on the Bryant Park story so I can pitch it to Dimi." She shook her head. "I keep coming back to those pictures I took, Tru. There's something so..." her voice trailed off "...so *odd* about them. I keep staring at them, feeling I'm missing something." She glanced at him. "Do you know how you feel when you can't think of a word? As if it's right on the tip of your tongue?"

He nodded, the sound of his voice, like his wine-dampened lips, lost in her hair. "Yeah. Sure."

"That's how I feel every time I look at those pictures. Anyway, I've got notes, tapes and photos to pull together for the PR piece. Once I start, I can see what kind of story we've got. Next week, I might interview your father and brothers. Maybe even talk to your mother again. I really like the family angle."

He had to fight not to react. Sure, Trudy needed to spend time in her office, but so did he, and it wouldn't hurt to use their assignment as an excuse to spend a few more days with each other, would it? Oh, she'd teased him about never being off-duty, but really it was she who didn't let go of the job. Taking a deep breath, he pressed her nearer, needing to feel her body join with his once more, and he sighed, blood tunneling to his groin at the contact. "Ah," he couldn't help but say, the teasing tone not concealing his emotions as much as he wished. "Is that what I am to you? An angle?"

She groaned. "We're in this together."

She made him sound unreasonable, but Trudy was distancing herself. Sometimes, when he touched her, he felt her move away, just slightly, and while he didn't want to acknowledge it, the truth was, he found it threatening. Deep down, he figured she'd get scared and run. It's what Sue had done. His heart couldn't take that again.

"I need to open up some more time," Trudy explained, the lightness of her tone not hiding her defensiveness, no more than her wheedling when she said, "C'mon. Don't you want to solve the Glass Slipper case?"

He refrained from asking how they'd solve it if they returned to their separate offices. "I've been questioning people all night."

"I know," she conceded.

He'd spent the early evening pounding the pavement while Trudy waited in the car. With her at his side, he feared he'd look suspicious. As it was, he'd established a cover as a foot fetishist, trying to sell pictures, so if proprietors saw him with a woman as clean-cut as Trudy, they'd suspect the worst. She turned thoughtful. "Maybe it's not a foot fetishist, after all, Truman."

He'd rather talk about what was happening between them. "Why else would a guy steal women's shoes?"

"Maybe there's a shoe design angle?"

There was that word again. *Angle.* Truman was tired of hearing it when they were up here alone, on a summer night, well-fed and enjoying a view of stars and city lights. Since Sue, he'd stopped thinking in romantic terms, but tonight, even the most hardened cynic would feel moved. What man could resist lounging on a rooftop in New York, staring at stars and skyline while aroused and holding a woman he desired? Right now, his body was clamoring for what only she could give. He couldn't see any angles at all. Just him and her. Nevertheless, he was a good cop, and she had a point, so he said, "A design angle?"

She nodded, her head brushing his chest. "Maybe this has to do with shoe designers, Tru. Those Madison Avenue fashion types get pretty competitive. And they're high profile."

He thought of the brutal murder of designer Gianni Versace on the steps of his Miami mansion, and of how his Upper East Side store had looked the next day, its windows draped in black. "There might be something to that." Fashion was big business and designers were household names, building vast empires from their investments. "I don't know, though. It doesn't make sense. This thief's stealing shoes, not designs for them."

"I'm just suggesting we might be assuming the

wrong motive," countered Trudy. "What's that called in logic?" She frowned. "You know, when you build an argument that makes perfect sense, but it crumbles because it's built on a faulty premise?"

He shrugged, strumming a hand up and down her back. "Beats me, but I get your point." He'd pinpointed Manhattan's most active foot fetishists, but they had solid alibis. The line of inquiry wasn't producing leads, so she was right; it was time to look elsewhere. Stroking her hair again, he ran his fingers beneath the strands, then smoothed them. "Shoe designers, huh?"

Snuggling, she clasped her hands on his chest, rested her chin in the valley of her fingers and stared up at him. When she spoke, her breath was as warm as the night. "Yeah. What do you think? I'm smart, huh?" She flashed him a smile.

"Brilliant," he agreed.

"Keep it up and you might get sex tonight."

"I'll be sure and remind you that you said that."

"Really," she said. "What do you think of my new theory?"

He shrugged. "I don't know, Tru."

He tried to train his mind on work, but he was thinking of how much his body had come to crave hers. Every inch of her was something he fed on, and the more he ate, the hungrier he got. Through her, he was coming to understand a violence within him he'd never even suspected was there. Deep down, he wanted her to experience the same hunger. He wanted her craving for him to be just as intense and overwhelming. Instead, she was talking about work. His throat constricted, and his hand raked possessively into her hair once more. Closing his fingers, he tilted up her face and watched the shadows play on her cheeks.

The city loomed all around them. Impenetrable monuments of marble lined the avenues, and modern structures of steel shot like bullets into the sky. Millions of people walked the streets below. But this high up, there was only the softness of her breath. Her eyes, usually so clear, looked smoky in the dark, just the way he'd imagined them on the day they'd met. *Eyes like smoke*, he thought, realizing he was the only man who'd ever seen her this unguarded.

He wanted more.

Oblivious of his thoughts, she sighed. "What other motive would someone have for stealing shoes?" Trudy asked rhetorically. "And what kind of person could gain access to those apartments? So many of the victims were wealthy with high-profile careers. Some even have live-in bodyguards."

His curse was soft, abrupt. "Dammit," he whispered, heat and urgency blinding him.

She stared at him. "What, Tru?"

"I don't want to talk about this," he returned, his tongue suddenly feeling thick in his mouth. He wanted to bind this woman to him. He wanted to lie naked with her, right this minute, and let their seeking bodies learn to further accommodate each other. He wanted to find every inch of common ground where they could exist together, as a man and woman.

He was astonished by the rush of his own need, the passion that wouldn't take no for an answer, the aching power of his desire. "With you lying on top of me," he said, coming to a sitting position before grasping her hand and quickly pulling her to her feet, "I can't think straight." Right now, crime could run rampant on the streets. Gunfire could sound next door. Truman didn't care. Leaning, he blew out the candles. He needed to be in bed with her now, naked with her wet and open beneath him.

She gestured. "But all our stuff..."

"Can wait."

Moments later, they were inside her apartment. He kicked the door shut and hauled her against him. "I've wanted you all day—" His voice was rough, his tongue still strangely heavy in his mouth, the words garbled. "I've needed to feel you..." Angling his hips snugly to hers, he moved so he could pleasure her through her clothes, beginning to build the rhythm. "To feel you like this..."

Her arms circled his neck, yielding, but not enough. His were so much greedier, wrapping around her so his hands could tunnel down her spine and over her backside. He groaned in agony, his itching fingers moving upward on the silk of the dress, the fabric flowing like water over his palms as he pushed the hem higher. Sucking a breath through clenched teeth, he throatily whispered, "Oh, Trudy," as silk gave way to the heart-stopping skin of her thighs.

"Bare skin," he commented mindlessly, wild when he discovered that more than her thighs was bare. She was wearing only a thong, and he shuddered, his hands caressing her exposed backside. Fondling, he rubbed brisk, warm circles on the cheeks, heating her skin before he spanked her lightly, nothing more than a love tap. When it made her moan, he spanked again, this time catching her bottom as she thrust upward, kneading the swell of the cheeks, his heart pounding.

Whispering nonsensical words, he found the string nestled in the crack, and played with it, lifting the slim wedge of watery silk so it caught in her parted cleft. Raising the string, he worked it so it rose and fell, and when she uttered a deep, shuddering sound, he strummed more aggressively, sliding the silk back and forth between her legs, knowing without touching that she drenched the fabric. Whimpering, she lost control and her body began to arch...

But she wanted to get away, too. She edged back. *Always away*, Truman thought illogically. He hated that she fought complete surrender. Each time, she held back...just a little. What made her shy away? He'd tried to love, and even though he'd gotten burned, he'd had countless relationships since Sue. It was only commitment he avoided.

This, he wanted. Trudy could run, but he was determined to catch her. He was every bit as ambitious as she. Difference was, his goal was to have her fully yield to him. Capturing and fierce, his mouth took hers possessively. Smothering her lips with his, he locked his mouth so tightly to hers that breath didn't pass. Her muted whimper was lost, his groan lost. What was found was the agonizingly soft touch of taut buds that strained, peaking against his chest. Her breath came in fits and starts as his hands swept around her back to support her.

Her knees nearly buckled as he started working the strap of the thong again. He fisted his free hand in silk and lifted the dress over her head in a gesture. For a second, he just stared. She was braless. Gorgeous. And then his mouth was on hers again. His eyes were shut, but his mind was still seeing her. She'd worn no slip. No bra. Just the G-string that threatened to make him explode. Just a slim strip of panty that covered hair she kept trimmed—and exposed all the rest. The sight of her naked breasts had been too much. Her flesh was so hot, rosy and aroused; the tender, succulent tips begged for more.

Her hands unbuttoned his shirt, smoothing his pectorals, stroking his nipples. Flicking his tongue rhythmically, he mimicked the slow grind of his hips as her hurried hands dropped, unbuckling his belt.

"Yes," he murmured. He wanted to be rid of his clothes.

A shaky whimper met his ears as she dragged down his zipper. He broke their kiss. His back hit the door. His chest heaved with breath, and he whispered, "no," because he wanted this to last, and he knew he'd come if she so much as touched him.

He didn't. But he lost his mind when her hand slid inside his briefs, pushing them down. He went madder still when her panties brushed his thigh. It was only a scrap of silk, but it burned him. "Trudy," he gasped hoarsely, the wood of the door mercilessly unforgiving on his back, his throat dry and his heart aching as he ducked again to kiss her hard, drowning in the feel of her lips, his mouth yearning, each drop of her taste enticing to the point of oblivion. A feast for the gods. And then he simply cried out. Her hands had found him. Freed him. His head reared back, his neck straining as warm dry hands caressed his swollen flesh. Oh, he'd taught her well, he thought in agony. He'd shown her exactly what he liked, how to tease him, how to keep him suspended on the brink.

Slowly, firmly, she squeezed, and he shuddered, the delicious sensations more than any man could stand. A shaky moan ripped through his whole body. It wracked his frame, and had him bracing his legs. Muscles leapt on his thighs, bunching and going taut. Raising his arms, he flexed his fingers, clasping his hands behind his neck, otherwise unsure what he'd do as she milked pleasure from every pore of his body.

"Don't tease me, Trudy," he gasped. He was desperate, even more so when she ignored his command and slowed the rhythm, obviously not caring about his overwhelming need for release, but keeping him hanging in space, consumed by need, his tortured body crying out. "Trudy," he warned hoarsely, knowing she was intentionally withholding the last touch he most needed.

"What?" she whispered innocently, barely stroking, her voice a pant.

Maybe he would have suffered it, but when she touched the tip, caught a drop of moisture and swirled, he abruptly broke contact, gently grasping her panties. He pulled down the senseless, flimsy string, groaning when he felt their dampness in his hand, nearly bursting when he registered the scent.

He didn't bother to further undress. The bed, only five feet away, was too far. He needed her. Like this. Now. As he lifted her, his jeans and briefs pulled across his braced thighs. He swiftly turned, bringing her legs around his hips. Pressing her back to the door, he entered her. He thrust too hard, too deep, and she gasped, but the wet passage enveloping him could take even more. He gave it, thrusting upward, burying himself, his open eyes blind, his mind hanging on to a last shred of control he wasn't about to lose, not until she gave as much as he. He drew back only long enough to see how her mouth had slackened with rapture. Her eyes were dark and smoky, glazed with lust, just the way he'd imagined them the first time they met. "Don't hold back, Trudy."

"What do you want from me?" she whispered.

"Everything."

"This is everything," she whimpered, her words strangely broken as she came, their import lost as he let go, too, a burst of wild heat pouring from him, the earth-shattering spasms shaking him to the core. She gushed around him, and he realized two things. They hadn't used protection, and he didn't give a damn.

Her voice was still coming on a whimper. "What do you want from me, Truman?"

Lowering her, he realized she was gathering her clothes, not bothering with the panties, but pulling the dress over her head again. Since he was in an awkward position, only half undressed, he followed suit, pulling his pants back up and zipping them. She looked upset. He knew then that he'd pushed her too hard, but he was only half sorry. He wanted more, and he wasn't going to pretend otherwise.

Eyes that had been smoky with lust, now looked watery, as if she was on the verge of tears, and suddenly, he imagined her floating away, like a balloon. He wondered what he'd do without her. Days ago, he'd been a rational man. It was a state of affairs that had ended the day he met Trudy Busey.

"I'm sorry," he apologized.

"Earlier, you didn't want to talk about work," she said, "and now, you're telling me I'm holding back."

He wanted to deny it, but since it was true, he leaned and cupped a hand around her shoulder. "I feel you pulling away from me," he murmured, his breath catching as he lifted a finger to stroke her face. "I won't hurt you, Trudy. Is that what you think? Is that what you're afraid of?"

She looked strangely lost, and it almost made him regret he'd said it. He liked to see her on top of her game and in control—she was so smart and strong—yet the closer they got, the more his presence seemed to strip away her natural confidence. It was as if the relationship that should have fed her strengths was draining them away.

"I need time." Looking exposed, she glanced away, her eyes darting toward the windows where the liquid sky opened on a million scattered stars. "I've never been with anybody, Tru. You know that. I told you that. I'm not used to this. Even at home, I kept to myself. My father and brothers had their own little mutual admiration society..."

Every part of him that didn't ache suddenly hurt even more. "Let me be your admiration society."

"I'm trying, but all my life, I've been alone..."

"I'm here now," he countered, wishing she could accept how good this was.

"I've let my other stories go. I'm behind at work. I've never been behind at work before."

"I support your work," he managed, trying not to panic, knowing she was slipping away. "I'm on your side, Trudy. You've got to believe that."

"I know you are. It's just that I—"

"Need time," he repeated. After what just happened between them, he really couldn't stand it. Maybe it was because Sue had left him so abruptly. Or because his youthful heart had ached so much after she miscarried. He'd been so innocent. He'd never even thought to worry about the practicalities of having babies—the finances, the possibility that something could go wrong. He'd concerned himself solely with the emotions of becoming a dad, dreaming of the rosy future he was about to share with a son or daughter. "I understand," he forced himself to say, taking a deep breath. "I'd better go."

"Not now," she whispered. "Not like this."

But he had to leave. Not for her, but for him. A long time ago, he'd given more of himself than another would accept, and it hurt too much. Maybe *he* needed time. Realizing his hand was already on the doorknob, he turned it and stepped across the threshold. "You're going into the office tomorrow," he said, glancing back into her apartment. "Will you be on the drive-along the next day?"

Her voice was strained. "I'm not sure. I've got so much work to do. I...I'll let you know."

"See you soon, Trudy." Leaning, he brushed a kiss across her cheek, his heart aching at the possibility that this might be the last time he ever saw her as a lover. As the door swung shut, he wished he wasn't noticing her eyes. Now the smoke in them wasn't about lust, it was about hurt. He tried not to think about it as he went downstairs, but he knew she was crying. He wanted to turn around, retrace his steps, return to her apartment and hold her again.

But he didn't.

"WHY'S HE BLOWING HIS cover?" Trudy whispered, feeling like a fool for following a man with whom she'd shared a bed. As she retied one of her sneakers, she kept her eyes riveted on Truman who was inside a sex shop, talking to a proprietor. Frowning, she watched him flash his badge. What was he up to?

Since she hadn't had the nerve to call him for three days, she'd begun tailing him again, and she was going to feel ridiculous if he caught her. Of course, she was prepared to tell him that her motivations were work-related. If he solved the Glass Slipper, she wanted the story. Yes, that's why she was following him just as before, buying items in stores and asking questions. This time, however, she was pretending to be his girlfriend's sister.

"I just want to break this story," she whispered. "That's all there is to it."

But it was a lie. She'd had to see Truman, if only at a distance. She missed his intelligence, his conversation, the casual, unconscious swagger of his walk, and the humor glinting in his eyes.

And sex.

She missed that most of all. She'd waited her whole life for the kind of physical relationship that was budding between her and Truman. But she couldn't handle the emotions, could she? She was too immature. Fighting self-loathing, she felt her heart ache, and she wished they had another scheduled PR precinct visit so she'd have an excuse to see him. For a brief moment in time, Truman Steele had been hers. Maybe he still was. Trudy didn't know, and she was too scared to find out, so she was avoiding him. She wasn't even sure what had happened, only that she'd wept for hours after

Truman left her apartment. Now she couldn't confront him until after the visit with her family tomorrow night. The thought of simultaneously dealing with her father, brothers and Truman was simply too much.

Excuses, her mind argued.

Sometimes, she wished she'd never met Tru, and that the most glorious week and a half of her life would vanish. She felt completely transformed. And yet, before this, life had been so simple. She'd been busy, trying to figure out how to make Dimi, her father and brothers take her seriously, and focusing her negative energies on Scott Smith-Sanker, who would scoop his own mother, and who therefore deserved everything he got.

Simple.

Until Truman came along. Hadn't she suspected that adding a Y chromosome to the carefully mixed cocktail of her life would produce something explosive? It hurt to admit it, but she didn't bond well with people, not on a deep level, she just didn't. Truman knew it, and he needed something more. Didn't that mean she should gracefully exit the picture?

Maybe she was one of those people destined to be alone, great at her job and dedicated to a career. Her heart ached, protesting. She didn't want to be alone! But she never seemed to understand the "something more" that people kept expecting of her.

Taking time for herself hadn't helped. Truman's absence only left a huge hole inside Trudy, waiting to be filled. With a sigh, she sat down on a stone wall and zipped up the hooded sweatshirt jacket she wore with jeans, then she propped a shopping bag beside her, sure no one would bother her. After the incident with

Leon and Alfredo, people in the park knew she had defenders. Glancing into the bag, her spirits further plummeted. Before, when she shopped, she'd been fantasizing about Truman. But now, she missed him...

Distracting herself, she tried to think about the lottery story. The assistant she'd talked to, Gracie Dale, seemed about to crack. She'd gone so far as to divulge that the winner was a housewife. But why would a housewife want to hide her good fortune? "Probably to hide a private fund her husband and kids wouldn't know about," Trudy whispered. Maybe the woman wanted to know she could vanish, flee the country and find complete freedom.

Trudy started, realizing she'd been picturing her own mother, not a stranger. Funny, she thought, how we project our own experience onto other people's lives. And then she realized something had drawn her from her reverie—his voice.

"If you want to know what I'm up to, Trudy," Truman said, his voice flinty, "Just ask. You don't have to skulk around, following me like this."

She rose quickly, not liking how he was towering over her, and needing to meet him head-to-head. She tried to ignore the racing of her heart. "I'm not skulking!"

It was barely discernable in the darkness, but more emotions were roiling around inside his eyes than Trudy could count. "You don't need to follow me," he repeated. She was about to respond when he curled a hand over her arm and added, "C'mon."

The contact made her knees weak. Only when he touched her did she fully understand the force of what she'd so long denied herself. Sex was far too powerful.

Pure dynamite. She never should have messed with it. It had bound her to Truman so quickly. Now she felt she couldn't live without him. She needed him. Emotionally, she'd opened herself to him, and maybe there was no turning back. "Where are we going?"

"I'm taking you home."

"I'M BEGINNING TO TAKE this personally,'" Trudy read, her assessing blue eyes scanning the note from Candy, which she'd snagged from under a windshield wiper. "'You need to call me, Officer. The sooner, the better.'" Glad for the distraction, Trudy glanced at Truman. "Another note from Candy."

"Thanks," he said gruffly.

"I wasn't really following you," she began, unable to tamp down her embarrassment once the cruiser started moving.

Truman's eyes stayed on the windshield as he guided them between yellow cabs, taking a straight shot downtown on Broadway, through heavy traffic. Under the lights—mostly from theater marquees and headlights—the cityscape was as bright as daylight. "Whatever happened to teaming up? To solving the case together? Remember? I make the arrest, and you get the story?"

Things had become so much more complex. Trudy glanced away from the windshield, tuning out the dispatch radio he'd left running. "I would have called before now, but after the way you left my apartment..."

He shot her a long glance, his eyes saying, *What choice did I have?* When the stoplight nearest Penn Station turned red, he uttered a frustrated groan. Braking, he glanced across the seat, and when their gazes meshed, her heart lurched. She'd never realized she could miss someone so much in just a few days. "You could have called me," he said. "Or come by the precinct."

She thought of the days she'd spent in the office, hedging whenever Dimi approached her. Other than the planned public relations stops at precincts slated for her and Truman in the future, she'd said she thought she had enough material to begin writing the article. "*You* could have called *me*," she countered.

"You're the one who needed time."

"I was going to call," she assured, keeping her voice calm and wondering what he'd do if he knew the depth of emotion she suspected had lain dormant and untapped inside her. What if, like a floodgate, something opened inside her and she needed him too much? She feared she'd be overwhelmed if she gave her whole self. Was that really what Truman wanted? Absolutely everything? What if you loved someone that much, and something happened to them...what if they died? Or left you? She pushed away the thoughts. "I was going to call you after the visit with my family this weekend, really Truman. I've...missed you."

"Is it really that hard to say?"

"No." She repeated the words firmly. "I missed you."

"You don't have to see your family alone, you know."

No, but she wasn't sure she was ready to have Truman meet them. "It'll be fine. I'm afraid I've given you the wrong impression. They're really nice people..."

"I've never doubted that." He traced the steering wheel with a finger, his expression thoughtful. "But just because they're nice in some ways doesn't mean you got what you needed from them, Trudy. And what you need is all that matters to me."

Wow. How many men really said things such as that? One in a million. Her breath caught. She wanted to believe him. "I know...I just..." Just what? Her mind raced for excuses, and when she found none, she sighed, then simply switched the topic. Avoidance. It was how Buseys handled knotty interpersonal situations. "I see you've got the patrol car tonight."

He nodded, not missing a beat, as if he hadn't even noticed the change in subject. "They didn't need it at the station."

"Weren't you afraid you'd blow your cover?" she asked, relieved he wasn't pressing her. "I saw you show your badge to the man in that store."

He shrugged, the light touch of his hand on the wheel giving a lie to the tension in his body. "None of the leads are panning out. You're right. There's another motive, which means I need to try another tactic."

The light hadn't yet changed and a stream of people were pouring into the intersection, mindless of the crosswalk. Truman turned, lightly grasping her sleeve. A spark came with the unexpected contact, and her heart softened. His eyes turned to liquid. "The other night, I shouldn't have left, Trudy."

True. But she hadn't wanted this turbulence in her life. She was so close to working on stories that might garner genuine respect from her father and brothers. *There are other men,* urged a voice inside her. When she turned back to Truman, he'd tilted his head, his slanted eyes making him look more sexy than any man had a right to. Before she could say anything more, the light changed. A horn sounded from behind them, and Truman turned his attention to the windshield.

She took a deep breath, wishing he didn't tie her in knots. As childish as it was, she was tempted to swing open the door at the next traffic light, get out and take the subway. But, of course, they didn't hit any more lights.

"You all but threw me out, Trudy," he continued.

Maybe. But not before she'd felt herself surrendering so much more than she'd known existed inside her. And still, that hadn't been enough for him. She'd been so confused. "I didn't throw you out," she defended, her voice low. "That's an exaggeration."

"You said you need time."

"Not forever."

"How much?"

"I don't know."

Frustrated, she stared at the colored patterns of light at play on the pavement, the winking red eyes of taillights, then white starbursts from headlights in the cross traffic. "Why can't we go back to how things were a week ago? We were having fun, making each other laugh, Truman."

"We were doing a hell of a lot more than that."

She nodded slowly. "Yeah. We were."

Lifting his eyes from the traffic, he stared across the seat. "I can't pretend this isn't happening, Trudy."

"It's all or nothing for you, huh?"

He sighed. "I guess it is."

But what could "all" mean, since they'd just met? One touch, and she knew they were like wild people who'd lost every scrap of common sense. Half the time, they were undressed before they even hit the sheets. But what now? She simply didn't know what the next step was. All she knew was that she felt alive for the first time in her life.

"We were going to team up," he reminded. "Solve this case together."

"The last time we were together, you said you didn't want to talk about the case."

"I wanted to talk about us," he admitted.

Us. Why couldn't he understand? She'd never relied on people, nor had the experience of an ongoing sexual relationship. She felt as if she'd been wrenched from darkness and plunged into the light. The transition was abrupt, but it felt so right, too. She could admit that much. Each moment in his arms, she felt she finally belonged somewhere, and that someone believed in her. She forced herself to point at the curb in front of her building. Having no idea what he expected, she said, "You can drop me off."

The only empty space was beside a fire hydrant, and since his fellow officers wouldn't ticket a cruiser, Truman pulled into it. Sighing, he shook his head as if trying to pinpoint where they'd gone wrong. "I don't want to drop you off, Trudy. I want to come inside and spend the night. Look—" He flexed his hands on the wheel again, his eyes lancing into hers. "I'm sorry I got mad earlier. The truth is, I hated seeing you running around down by Bryant Park. It's dangerous there."

She struggled not to react to the protectiveness. "My job takes me dangerous places."

"The mayor's office? Cruising with me?"

Instinctively, she knew he was pushing her buttons, spoiling for a fight that would either drive her into his arms again, or away from them. Whatever middle ground they were traversing was just too uncomfortable. "You're patronizing me."

Suddenly reaching, he closed a hand over her shoulder, cupping it. "Maybe I am," he conceded. "But I'm a cop. I'm out here every day. I arrest lowlifes. Murderers and thieves." He pointed through the windshield. "If you know where to look, there's danger everywhere."

As far as she was concerned, the danger wasn't but two feet away from her, and his name was Truman Steele. "I'm a reporter. I'm out here every day, too. And you're being absurd."

"See that one guy?" Truman continued as if he hadn't heard. "He's a runner. And the other guy at the end of the block? He's the lookout. The guy in the middle's selling something." Truman shrugged. "Who knows what? I should probably go find out, but right now, you're more important. Trudy, these guys are out here every night."

"I live here!" she exploded. "You don't think I notice?"

"You're so pretty," he whispered now, his voice crumbling, his eyes going as soft as the velvet night. The hand on her shoulder gentled, his thumb probing into the hollow near her collarbone, sending and seeking warmth through her jacket.

"Okay," she conceded, her heartbeat quickening, either with the contact or barely restrained temper, she wasn't sure which. "I'm pretty, Truman. And blond. Petite. Blue-eyed." She stared at him, her voice hard with banked emotion. "But I'll repeat what I said the first day we met. Looking like this doesn't make me lack brain cells."

He looked stunned. "That's not what I meant. You're the smartest woman I know, Trudy."

"And despite that, you like to envision me covering stories about the zoo? Or architecture in the city?" She shook her head. "They say people are attracted to the familiar. Well, you're definitely like my father."

"I'm not your father."

"I said you're *like* him."

As the tips of his fingers tightened on her jacket, his voice grew husky. "I'm guilty of wanting to protect you. Maybe I couldn't stand it if anything happened to you. Did you think of that?"

The words made her ache, but she wasn't backing down. "I can't live my life in a vacuum. Don't you know what that does to people?" Suddenly, the words were coming on a force of their own, and fierce pain threatened to shatter her veneer. "Don't you know how overprotection drives people away? How it makes them want to run?" She gripped the shopping bag, her fingers curling around the handle, then she grasped the handle of the car door.

His eyes searched hers as if he realized anything he might say would be wrong. "I don't want to push you away, Trudy. Dammit, that's the last thing I want."

"I want to succeed," she continued, barely hearing. "Make something of myself."

"I know. I can help you."

"So you say," she volleyed, pushing open the door and stepping to the curb. Turning, she stared at Truman, keeping her hand on the ledge of the window for balance. "As long as I'm under lock and key by nightfall. That's why my mother left. She couldn't stand feeling trapped. Do you know what she said when I was born?''

Truman stared at her a long moment, then shook his head.

Trudy had never known how good it could feel to get this out of her system. ''She said she'd never wanted a girl, because in the town where I grew up that meant your life was over. There weren't job opportunities. She started her career at my father's paper, and got nothing but grunt work. He patronized her, married her, and then expected a big, whopping thanks when he gave her a pink slip, so she could better raise the kids.''

Truman's intuitive, whiskey-colored eyes were trained on her like a light. When he spoke, his voice was utterly calm. ''When did she leave?''

Realizing she'd said too much, Trudy stared at him from where she was wedged in the door. ''Who?''

''Your mother.''

But she was already moving, wanting to get inside the apartment before she fell apart, and wishing she'd never met Truman Steele. The man was far too probing. Right before she slammed the car door, she muttered, ''The day I was born.''

TRUMAN STARED THROUGH the windshield. Each time he was sure he'd figured out Trudy, she tossed in a wrench. Now his anger felt thoroughly unjustified. The truth was, he'd left her apartment days before because he didn't want to give more of himself than Trudy. Like a fool, he'd been running an emotional tally, determined not to replay his history with Sue.

But she wasn't Sue. His heart twisted inside his chest. How could he have been so blind? Oh, he'd known Trudy's father and brothers hadn't supported her career enough, but why hadn't he noticed how she'd opened up with his mother, thriving on the maternal attention?

"Because Ma always has that effect on people," he muttered. At one time or another, half the big, tough cops in New York had cried on Sheila Steele's shoulder.

But Trudy's mother had abandoned her family. Even worse, she'd done so the day Trudy was born. What was Truman supposed to do now? He recalled his mother labeling Trudy ambitious, and how Trudy had glowed under the praise. All the while, he'd assumed the mother she'd never mentioned had died.

"Never assume," he whispered.

That was rule number one. He was too good a cop to assume anything. Nothing at crime scenes was ever as it appeared. And in the course of his job, he'd talked with countless kids who felt abandoned. He should have recognized the signs in Trudy. As far as Truman was concerned, making a kid feel unloved ranked right up there with the worst kind of crime. His mind was churning with questions. Had her mother stayed in Milton, or gone elsewhere? Had she kept in touch? Or had Trudy contacted her and been rejected? Maybe the woman had simply vanished...

And what of Trudy's brothers? Did they blame their sister, since their mother left home after her birth? Was that the root of her trouble with them? "How could a woman leave a newborn," he murmured, even though he knew the answers—many sympathetic, but all tragic. The Busey men had probably clung to Trudy, terrified she'd leave. Instead of feeling loved, she'd felt stifled, and she'd done exactly what they feared—plotted an escape to New York.

"But who knows?" So far, every guess he'd made about Trudy was wrong. There was only one way to find out the truth—ask.

A moment later, he was knocking on her door. She didn't answer, but he knew she was there. Leaning, he brought his lips to the crack in the door. "Trudy?" He knocked harder. "I know you're home. C'mon. Open up."

A minute passed. "Trudy, I'm not leaving."

"Go away."

If that's what she really wanted, he would, but deep down, he thought she needed him. He hoped, anyway. "Please, Trudy."

Finally, the door swung open and she stepped back to admit him. She'd been crying, and now she was holding her blue eyes open too wide as if that might keep him from noticing the red rings rimming them.

"I don't want to talk about any of this," she said simply.

At least she was honest. Letting instinct guide him, he kept his eyes fixed on her a long moment. Then he did the last thing she'd expect. He offered an encouraging smile, his gaze drifting over her, his heart aching with what had to be love. Truman had never felt anything quite like it, except maybe for the baby he'd never had. This was different, but the emotions ran deep. "I'm glad," he assured, hoping she'd talk later if he gave her the time she needed. "Because that's not why I came up."

She didn't look the least bit convinced. "No?"

He shook his head. "No," he repeated, his eyes still roving over her. She looked adorable in the threadbare jeans, sweatshirt jacket and beat-up sneakers. Her face was scrubbed clean, since she'd cried off what little makeup she'd worn. He'd never wanted to hold her more than at that moment. He refrained, determined not to scare her off again. Shrugging, he nodded toward the bag she'd carried in from the car. "I just happened to notice you went shopping again tonight, and before you got out of the car, I forgot to ask what was in the bag."

A small, tentative smile curled her lips, and as glad as Truman was to see it, the relief in her eyes hurt. Would she realize she could safely share her innermost self? "Well," she said. "That's a question I might be able to answer..." She paused a heart-stopping second, then added his nickname. "Tru."

His heart tugged, his groin pulled, and right then, Truman knew he'd settle for any tiny piece of her. He smiled. "I'm on pins and needles."

"Sounds uncomfortable."

"It is."

"I guess you can come inside then."

But he was already inside, leaning against the door where they'd last made love. For a moment, they merely stood there staring at each other, and then she sighed and stepped into his embrace, wreathing her arms around his neck. "I'm sorry," she apologized, her voice choked. "I don't know what I'm doing."

"I know," he whispered, wrapping his arms around her and stroking her hair. "But do you want to know a secret?" When she nodded, he said what his mother always had. "Nobody knows what they're doing when it comes to relationships. They're always new. Every time. And this one between you and me—" He paused, just long enough to tilt her face up to his and brush a chaste kiss to her lips. "It's special, Trudy. Really special. That's bound to make it doubly confusing."

A smile worried her mouth. "If I didn't like you so much, it would make things easier," she confessed. "I wouldn't be so scared."

But then he wouldn't be here, holding her. "You're right about something else, too," he soothed. "We've been together a lot. We've been having great sex."

Her eyes were hot on his. "Is it great?"

She didn't have anything to compare it to. "The best," he assured. "Even if it wasn't, which it is, it would be hard to adjust to if you're not used to having somebody."

"I want to adjust," she whispered mournfully.

"I know," he whispered back, relief filling him as he drew her tightly to his body and pressed his whole length against her, infusing her with his warmth. "But beneath fear there's always hurt," he schooled. Gazing down, he gave her a smile. "C'mon. I've got these big burly shoulders, and I hate having them go to waste, Tru. Feel free to cry on my shoulder."

"I'm not sure I can cry on command."

"I have faith in you," Truman said.

A moment later, when he squeezed her closer, she gave in and allowed herself to weep.

WHEN TRUMAN AWAKENED the next morning, missing the heat of her body against his, the first thing he noticed was Trudy, rummaging through his jeans pockets. "Hey, what are you doing?" Somehow, he managed to keep the tone nonconfrontational, but he was worried. He hadn't removed the letter from the lottery board from the inside pocket of his jacket. His mother had claimed the winnings, but because she'd named her sons as potential beneficiaries, the board was informing them each of tax-related issues.

Tossing off the covers, he rose and strode toward Trudy, trying to seem unconcerned. Playfully, he caught her hand, opening it on the contents of his pocket, figuring that if she'd found the letter, she'd have said something already.

"Sorry for snooping," Trudy said guiltily, primly turning, naked save for an open robe of transparent turquoise fabric.

"I couldn't be mad when you look like this," he assured, since he'd only been worried about the lottery correspondence.

"When I look like what?" she challenged, offering a smile as brilliant as the early morning sunshine coming through the window. "This sounds like something you should elaborate on."

"Like when you've stepped from a scented bath smelling like heaven," he clarified. He liked her without makeup, too. Her lips were wide, naturally pink, and against her pale skin, her mouth and eyes leapt out. Leaning, he pressed two matching kisses to her eyelids, then drew back, his gaze drifting over her wet hair. The lines of a comb were still visible. Stepping closer, his naked body grazed hers, and he gazed into her palm, further studying the items from his pocket.

"I was just thinking it might be interesting," she explained, "for the article about the NYPD. Suddenly, I wanted to know what cops carry in their pockets."

She was dead serious, and he found himself touched by the outrageous curiosity that drove her, and which he'd benefited from in bed. "It *is* an odd collection of stuff," Truman admitted, staring down at the items resting on her palm: a rabbit's foot, a whistle, mace. "The pocket watch belonged to my great-grandfather," he said, pride touching his voice. "He was the first Steele to become a cop. He carried it as a reminder that God never takes us before our time, not even if we spend every day in the line of fire."

"See," she said. "The contents of your pockets are more interesting than you know. A banker would carry completely different things."

"Yeah," he teased, momentarily forgetting about the letter from the lottery board and his mother's winnings. "More money."

She tweaked his side playfully. "Be serious, Tru."

He chuckled, her heat and scent too much for him. "I'm very serious," he assured. And very aroused. "Let's see what reporters have in their pockets." Slipping his hands inside her open robe, he glided them around her waist, then frowned. "What?" he murmured, humor in his eyes as he caressed her hips, molding his palms over warm skin. "No pockets?"

Trudy's eyes twinkled. "No, but I like the way you do research."

"Chalk it up to curiosity," he returned, his voice husky as he brought his hands upward, lifting a breast that peaked at his touch. Leaning, he suckled, loving the sharp sound of her audible breath. When he withdrew, he could see the pulse at her neck. He planted a kiss where it vibrated, filling his lungs with her scent and that of strong coffee. "A specialty blend you got at the Puerto Rican Import Company on Bleeker Street?" he guessed.

She grinned. "You don't need it. You feel pretty awake."

"Whatever you had in your pockets before..." he murmured "Must still be in the bed, Trudy. We'd better go look."

"You think a smart girl like me would fall for an old trick like that?"

"I was hoping."

She glanced toward the futon. "As long as you're only interested in finding lost items."

"I swear my motives are pure."

Once more, he lifted the hand cupped around the trinkets from his pocket. Opening her palm, he removed the things one by one, then pressed a kiss where they'd been. He turned her hand, studying the creases.

Her breath caught with anticipation. "You read palms?"

"Sure." His gaze caught hers. Eyes sparkling with humor became sober when he thought of last night. She'd cried, letting him hold her, her emotions as open to him as her body. Later, she'd told him that her mother had simply taken a suitcase and left the day she was born. Marcia Busey had moved out west and gone back to school, getting advanced degrees in journalism and fulfilling her professional dreams. Now, she worked as a talking head for a TV station in Birmingham. Trudy was the only child who'd ever voiced a desire to contact her, hoping to arrange a meeting, but her father had forbidden it. By the time she realized she didn't need his approval, years had passed and she'd lost her nerve. The closest she'd come to finding her mother was to track down her whereabouts and watch tapes of her news broadcasts. Well, maybe Trudy had been right not to pursue the matter, Truman thought now. If Marcia Busey had wanted to, wouldn't she have contacted her children?

The soft rasp of Trudy's voice drew him from his reverie. "So, what's my future hold?"

He shook his head gravely, his eyes warming once more. "To be honest, Trudy, I see a lot of sex in your future."

From the way her eyelashes fluttered, it was clear she was amenable to the idea. "Very far in the future?" she queried, feigning concern.

He peered hard, tracing a line in her palm. "Before work this morning."

She laughed. "That soon? Before or after coffee?"

Before he settled his lips on hers, he said, "Before. Your partner would rather be awakened the old-fashioned way."

A wicked glint appeared in her eyes, and as she pressed her hands down his naked torso, she murmured, "Like I said, my partner already seems awake to me."

For a moment, he merely enjoyed how she looked. Her robe was open, and sunlight and shadows danced across her breasts in lacelike patterns. Perky pink nipples peeked out, as if from the fancy underwear she favored. Tugging her the few feet to the futon, his mouth found her neck again, and using every inch of his tongue, he looped long wet kisses all the way down it, his hand once more cradling a breast, his ears reveling in the moan he provoked. Lowering his hand, he lightly tested the weight before deeply massaging her.

"This feels good," she whispered simply, lying back.

"It's going to feel better," he assured, his eyes soaking up the vision of her milky thighs slowly parting, quivering as she offered him access. His hand covered her there. Bending, he suckled an erect nipple, and as he pulled gently, he knew he'd never get enough of this taste. Their nights together were slowly bringing them to a place where he wouldn't be able to live without her.

"Get on top," he whispered.

"You like aggressive women, don't you?"

"Yeah. It's my one weakness."

Pulling her toward him, he gazed up at her as she straddled him, landing just inches from where he was hard. A shaky breath came from his parted lips as he registered the strength in her body, how her knees bracketed his sides. "Don't tease me," he warned. "I'm putty in your capable hands."

Her gaze swept down his torso, then stopped, leaving him awash in heat. A playful smile curled her lips. "You look pretty capable yourself right now."

He couldn't play anymore. His chest was too tight, his breath too shallow. All he could say was, "Hurry, Trudy."

The playful humor, so evident in her blue eyes, was replaced by vulnerability that moved him deeply. So serious now, she was going to try her best to make their joining meaningful...for him, for them. Reaching, he brushed a palm to her breasts once more, his eyes never leaving hers as she mounted him. Sweet, hot and wet, she slowly glided onto his length, stealing whatever breath was left in his body. He started to say he loved her then.

But her hips began to move.

8

AT FIRST TRUDY COULDN'T identify what had awakened
her, but her eyes opened, and when she inhaled, the
scent of coffee knifed to her lungs. She'd fallen asleep
again! She was late for work! Groaning, she tossed off
the covers and darted her eyes to the clock, relief flooding her. *It's only seven o'clock. Still plenty of time to get to
the* News *by nine.* Before she met Truman, she'd always
gone in early, but today...

Hey, she thought. *If I work my tail off this morning,
maybe I can hook up with Truman this afternoon and ride
along in the cruiser.* She had enough material for the article about the NYPD, but she'd enjoy spending the day
with Truman. Why not? Dimi didn't have to know it
wasn't strictly business. *Let somebody else cover the next
baby gorilla born at the Central Park Zoo or today's celebrity
auction at Sotheby's,* she thought with a lack of malice
that surprised her. The truth was, she'd never once
played hooky.

Hugging the pillow, she brought her knees to her
chest, curling into a nice, snuggly ball as she stared at
the sunlight streaming through the curtains. *Only seven
o'clock.* Truman had been gone less than an hour. Despite that, her body still felt him. Strong arms were still
wrapped around her and huge warm hands were still
exploring her, the touch assured yet tender. Last night,

he'd loved her deeply, but not before holding her a long time while she cried.

It was a first. As a kid, when she got upset, her father would concentrate on hiding his helplessness, then tell her to "buck up," or "keep a stiff upper lip," and because her tears had threatened Ed's and Bob's masculinity, the urge to reach out made them feel like sissies. When she'd needed her brothers most, they'd only teased her.

Truman was another breed. Trudy wasn't sure how she'd discovered it: Maybe it was the tenderness in brown liquid eyes that saw so much, or the melting touch of fingertips that guided her ever closer, or how he'd come to her apartment last night, not demanding to know about her mother, but pretending he'd come to see her purchases. With the smallest gestures, he kept signaling he could give her what she needed on an emotional level. *And last night, I let him get just a little closer.*

Feeling oddly proud of herself, Trudy smiled. She let her eyes drift shut again, deciding it wouldn't hurt her to sleep some more. "Just this once," she whispered. Didn't she deserve to take time to process the changes Truman was bringing into her life? Besides, the way he'd loved her body this morning had zapped her strength, which was why, as soon as he'd gone home to change clothes for work, she'd allowed herself the unusual luxury of staying in bed.

"Maybe you should keep an extra uniform at my place, Officer," she'd suggested after they'd made love and he was preparing to leave.

"Afraid I won't come back?"

It had been hard, but she'd chosen to take his words

seriously and admit the truth of it. She'd curled next to him in bed. "I'd miss you if you didn't."

"All the cops in Manhattan couldn't keep me away," he'd promised. "The first thing I'll do when I solve the Glass Slipper case is bring that slipper here and see if it fits you."

He'd started making more frequent allusions to claiming her, and she found it unsettling. Keeping things light, she'd rolled her eyes. "Asking me to marry you again?"

His gaze had become watchful. "Will you?"

Her heart had lurched. When he teased like this, he seemed so serious, but marriage was nothing to joke about. "There's not really a glass slipper."

"How do you know?"

"I read your files," she'd reminded. "And studied all the pictures of the stolen shoes."

"Maybe the theft of a glass slipper was unreported. And anyway," he'd added, "it was you who dubbed the case the Glass Slipper. If there's no glass slipper, why'd you do it?"

"Because I'd rather assume Prince Charming, not a foot fetishist, is the perpetrator." She'd frowned. "What was the case called before I renamed it, anyway, hotshot?"

"Case number 28974-11."

"Fancy name," she'd commented. "Shows imagination."

"No," Truman had corrected, rolling on top of her, his eyes glinting wickedly as he grasped her wrists, loosely circled them with his fingers and pushed them above her head. "*This* shows imagination." He'd glanced down, between their joined bodies, taking in the curves of her hips and breasts. "Are you sure it's really my uniforms you want to keep here?" he'd teased in playful seduction. "Or are you only after my handcuffs?"

She'd recalled the night Truman used them, so inventively latching her wrists to the leg of the bedside table. Gripping her hands around the smooth wood and holding tight, she'd felt the chill of metal on her skin, but she'd known it was all for show. He'd set her free anytime she desired, so she'd surrendered herself to him and the fantasy that he'd kidnapped her, forcing her to submit to his every whim.

"Your handcuffs?" She'd shaken her head in mock disdain. "Metal," she'd pronounced decisively, unable to believe how much fun Truman could be in bed. "Cold." Her eyes had narrowed. "Just like your heart."

Truman's legs had settled more comfortably between hers, so she'd been able to feel how aroused he'd gotten from the pillow talk. When her eyes widened, registering his readiness, he'd huskily charged, "You loved every minute of it, Trudy."

She had, but she primly countered, "I'll have you know, I've visited certain..."

He'd leaned for a kiss. "Certain...?"

"Establishments," she'd finished. "Shops," she'd added.

"Shops that carry certain..." he'd dangled the sentence just as she had, then dropped the word "...*items?*"

A thrill had moved through her as she thought of all the toys they'd played with. "Exactly. Which is why I know they make *fur-lined* handcuffs. Yours are inferior."

All her teasing was making him suffer, and determined to make the experience truly unbearable, she'd arched, moving so he was poised to enter her. He'd grunted softly, sucking in a breath as he'd moved his hips, creating an electrifying friction as the ready part of him touched where she waited. Fire had burst through her.

"You find fur-lined cuffs superior?"

Even though she was going out of her mind with desire, she'd managed to lift her nose in the air. "Infinitely."

"If you're good, I'll pick some up on the way home."

She'd giggled. "And if I'm bad?"

"Punishment."

She'd laughed. "I won't be satisfied until I see those fur-lined handcuffs hooked to your belt." Imagining him arresting hardened criminals with them made them both laugh. "Yes. I want to see you arrest people with them. I mean," she'd corrected, "People other than me."

"No way." He'd shaken his head. "If I started doing that, crime would skyrocket. People would *want* to get arrested."

He'd been laughing when he entered her, and the sound had bubbled inside her. When he'd kissed her again, he was kissing a smile, and she'd opened further...

Now she groaned. There'd been a knock at the door! *That's* what had awakened her earlier. "Who could it be...?" A grin widened her mouth. *Truman!*

Of course! He'd showered and changed, then come back for a kiss goodbye, since she'd planned to spend today at the office, pulling together information she'd collected for various articles. Her heart missed a beat. Maybe he was bringing over some of his uniforms now. Pushing aside questions about whether she was really ready for that, she murmured, "Or maybe he wants more of a send-off than a kiss." Her mind mulled over how to deliver it. Laughing softly, she tossed off the covers, then hopped out of bed, naked. "Coming," she called out. "Be right with you!"

She glanced around the room. "What a mess!" she muttered, a flush spreading over her skin from head to toe. She and Truman had turned this place into a major den of iniquity. It was amazing to see how quickly a transformation from virgin to vamp could occur. "The feather boa," she decided, absently talking to herself. "Oh!" she added. "And that old-fashioned corset!" She'd found it in one of the classier shops, and she'd been saving it. This was the perfect time to wear it!

She was wide-awake now, but she tried to sound sleepy when she called, "I'm on my way! Can you give me a minute?"

Just the thought of making love to him—hard, fast and quick—had her heart racing. Wrenching open a drawer, Trudy fished for the outfit. "I put it right here!" she whispered. "I know I did." Frowning, she lifted out pairs of new panties, carelessly tossing them over her shoulder, not caring where they landed. Finding a particularly creative pink G-string, she studied the slim triangle of silk covered with a tuft of pink feathers.

"No," she whispered, rejecting them. "Be right there!" she assured as the pink G-string arched over her shoulder, landing on top of the answering machine. "Ah, there you are," she whispered. Tugging a red lace corset around herself, she swiftly laced it so that her breasts tumbled from old-fashioned, conical lace cups. After rummaging in a jewelry box, she tied a black velvet choker around her neck, then slipped on black seamed stockings, affixing them to dangling garters. On her way to the door, she grabbed the feather boa, quickly slung it around her neck and slipped into black come-love-me pumps. Catching a glimpse of herself in a mirror, she felt a rush of excitement. She looked great.

"What?" she teased, swinging the door open wide and stepping back to admit him. "Did you bring those fur-lined handcuffs?"

There was a long pause.

Her heart seemed to drop to her feet, and all the wind left her chest in a rush. She'd been so sure it was Truman, she hadn't looked through the peephole. *Oh, Trudy, you're in New York City,* she thought. *Never open a door without looking first! You know better! This could have been muggers!*

It was definitely a mistake Trudy wouldn't make again.

At least it wasn't Dimi or Scott, but all the members of her family who'd frozen in the doorway were gaping at her. First, there was her father, Terrence Busey, a tall, rail-thin man with thinning gray hair. His mouth was slack, his blue eyes bugging, and because his hands were tightly gripped around the lapels of his own conservative tweed suit jacket, he looked as if he was fighting with himself, pretending to be his own opponent. Trudy half expected him to suddenly draw back a fist and slug himself in the jaw. Next came Bob and Ed, who were younger versions of her dad, wearing navy and khaki suits respectively. Their wives— gripping shopping bags, wearing shoes with bows on the toes, and wide fabric headbands—automatically pasted smiles on their faces.

Her sister-in-law, Kate, the blonde, cleared her throat numerous times, an automatic smile stretching her lips. She spoke first, saying, "Oh, hon, I think we might have come at a bad time."

Sherry, Ed's wife, nodded very, very slowly, as if she'd just discovered her head was made of glass and would break if she opened her mouth. She was a perky brunette, with brown eyes that were blinking rapidly as if to dispel the vision before her. Suddenly, her smile broadened to a grin. It was the same grin she'd mastered while shaking pom-poms and doing splits on the fifty-yard line when Ed was still a quarterback for the Milton Mountain Cats. "I think we've come at a bad time!" Sherry exclaimed brightly, looking stunned as she craned her neck to include Ed in her gaze. Offering an abrupt, horsey laugh, she giddily repeated, "We've come at a bad time! Oh, dear, didn't you just say that, Kate? Or am I imagining things?"

Trudy only wished she was imagining things. "No," she assured, "Kate *did* say that." And then she started edging slowly backward, wondering if she should hide in the bathroom until her family left. "Uh, hi," she managed to add, casting a quick glance down at her outfit, praying she was covered.

The red fabric concealed more of her than they'd see in a bathing suit. Nevertheless, her family was still crowded in the doorway, neither advancing, nor retreating. At any second, neighbors would begin emerging from their apartments to join the crowd. This being

New York, they'd assume Trudy had been murdered. She could almost hear the ruckus: Did anybody call an ambulance? Dial 911! Does the lady in 12-B need CPR?

The phone rang.

All eyes shifted from Trudy's outfit to her living quarters, but instead of the phone, they found racy panties strewn about, an issue of *Penthouse* creased open to the letters she and Truman had been reading each other. At least other various sundries were safely tucked away in a drawer, but unfortunately, the pictures of Truman were visible, and he was standing in front of every dirty bookstore in the city.

"He's really a nice guy," Trudy said in a rush, unable to believe this was happening. "He's a *cop*," she added, and then, since she was met by only blank stares, "A police officer. My *boyfriend*," she emphasized, vaguely wondering if she'd ever mentioned that term in front of her family. "He's a cop, on a case, that's why he's standing in front of all those stores..."

Her rambling had no effect. All eyes had landed on the answering machine. From beneath the G-string covered in pink feathers, a red light was blinking.

"I'd better get the phone!" Trudy managed brightly. It was only five feet away, but given what she was wearing, she didn't feel comfortable turning and strutting toward it. She stepped backward instead. *Almost within reach,* she thought.

"We called," her father said stoically, staring where the red light blinked through the panties.

"I can see that now. I should have played the messages, I really should have," she managed. "But I got in late and—" Suddenly thinking the better of detailing last night's activities, she changed tactics and said, "I can explain."

As if they feared Trudy really *would* start to explain, everyone started talking at once, and Trudy shot another anxious glance at the phone, which was on its fifth ring. Since there was already a call on the machine, it would pick up after six rings, not ten. Because she was often busy, developing photos, she'd set the ringer high. Cursing the day she hadn't changed to voice mail, preferring to screen her calls, she thought *Surely it's Dimi. Please, fate, be kind. Just this once let him be calling with the big lead he keeps promising. If only Dad would hear it...*

"We thought you might want to have breakfast," Sherry was saying cheerily, her eyes bugging.

"Just a crazy, spur of the moment idea," added Ed.

"You know, before you went to work, sis," said Bob.

"But we can see you're, uh, really busy," put in Kate.

Trudy's smile was starting to hurt. The machine picked up. She waited for her message to play, then for Dimi's familiar voice, rough from coffee and strong foreign cigarettes. *Hey, Trudy. How's the best reporter in the biz? Just want to let you know you needn't come into the News for any new assignments this morning because I'm calling with another hot tip, one I want you to pursue right away!* That's what Dimi was going to say.

In reality Truman's playful voice said, "Good morning, sexpot. I just called because they're out of those fur-lined cuffs. But I found some other things you might like. For instance—"

Whirling, Trudy snatched up the phone. As her fingers curled around the receiver, she realized her palms were slick with sweat. Her heart was palpitating. She cleared her voice until she found it. "My family's here," she whispered hoarsely.

Fortunately, Truman, being the intuitive man he was, understood the whole picture immediately, but she'd never forgive his chuckle. "I don't want to ask what you're wearing."

Her mouth was bone dry. "No," she agreed. "You don't."

He had the nerve to laugh. "Why didn't they call first?"

She stared at the blinking light on the machine. "They did," she said shortly, through gritted teeth.

"Do they still want to have dinner tonight?"

She could feel them staring at her back. Ten holes, one for each of their eyes, burned into the red fabric that did, at least, cover her backside. "I haven't asked," she said, wishing her voice didn't sound so strained. "Not yet."

"Here's what you do," Truman schooled. "Hang up, and calmly tell them we'll meet them at seven. Jen Pang's in Chinatown. No arguments. It's on the corner of Baxter and Canal Streets."

We. She thought about it. She wasn't ready for this, but given what was happening right now, she needed his support. "Will you be meeting us there?" she asked, capitulating. "Or coming to my place first?"

"Coming there first, of course. Those fur-lined handcuffs," he said. "Remember?"

She almost smiled. Just hearing his voice calmed her. "Okay," she agreed simply. Doing as he instructed, she hung up, turned around, and then one by one, she met the astonished gazes. "I'm so sorry I was unavailable to take your call last night," she explained, striving for a casual tone and reminding herself that her private parts really were covered. "Anyway, that was a friend of mine. He suggests we meet at Jen Pang's in Chinatown at seven tonight. It's on the corner of Baxter and Canal." Pausing, she took a deep breath. "Sorry," she added, "but meantime, you'll have to excuse me. I really need to get to work."

"Of course!" said Kate, looking relieved for the excuse to leave and tearing her gaze away from the panties. "We understand."

"Only too well! We can see you're busy!" exclaimed Sherry, shooting Trudy an impressed glance of frank appraisal, as if to say her little sister-in-law certainly knew how to please a man.

A moment later, as she shut the door behind them, Trudy found herself feeling strangely light-headed. For just a second, the black high heels she wore seemed to float above the floor. "I'll never forget the looks on their faces," she whispered, a laugh bubbling in her throat.

Giddily, she tried turning an impulsive circle, then another, her heels clicking on the hardwood floor. Seconds later, she was still whirling, spinning around until she finally collapsed, falling on her back in bed, her head swimming. Soft feathers from the boa bunched around her face, teasing her cheeks, and when she drew her knees to her chest, she crossed her ankles, the heels of her shoes clicking. For a moment, she could barely catch her breath. Oh, it was naughty of her, and she truly wished her father hadn't seen her apartment, but he was a world-weary reporter who'd get over it. One thing was certain, though: Her family would never see her in the same way again.

The phone rang. Laughing, she lifted it. "Hello?"

With her luck, it really would be Dimi this time, missing his chance to redeem her by mere minutes. Truman said, "Are you alone now?"

She released a sigh, and before she told him what had happened, simply said, "Yeah, thanks."

"For?"

"Calling me," she said, "at the exact right moment."

"Well," he said, "from everything I've heard, we need to come up with a game plan before dinner tonight."

We. Trudy was starting to like the sound of it. "Game plan?"

"THIS COULDN'T BE MORE perfect, Truman," Trudy whispered that night. "You're brilliant."

Truman answered by squeezing her knee as he leaned back in a red leather booth at Jen Pang's. Her brother, Ed, had just made a big show of placing his credit card on top of the exorbitant check and sending the waiter to the cashier with it, and now Truman was waiting patiently for Jen Pang to reject it.

Today, after spending the morning working at their respective jobs, he and Trudy had played hooky. Parking the cruiser, they'd shopped in Soho until they'd found the black, gold-trimmed cocktail dress Trudy was wearing with black hose and gold pumps. Later, when Truman arrived wearing a suit, with an extra uniform in tow, he'd talked her into pulling her hair into a French twist.

"You're gorgeous," he whispered now, watching her open a fortune cookie. She looked every inch the sophisticated New York professional and, for hours, he'd been enjoying the envious glances of her sisters-in-law. They were classy ladies in their own right, but Trudy was the one drawing eyes. Especially his.

"I will meet the man of my dreams," she quipped, reading the fortune.

Truman caught a loose tendril of her hair between his fingers and, as he replaced it against her neck, he savored the touch of smooth skin. Reading over her shoulder, he corrected, "What it really says is that the wheel of fortune is about to turn in your favor."

"Same difference."

"I'm glad you think so." He smiled, thinking of the lottery letter in the inner pocket of his suit jacket. Trudy's nearly finding it prompted him to fill out the form he'd been sent, but in all the excitement today, he'd forgotten to mail it. Now he reminded himself to drop it in a box, and to remove the note his mother had included when she'd passed it on. "Dreams of money don't ring your chimes?" he asked Trudy. "Only romance, huh?"

"Well," corrected Trudy, "money's always welcome."

"And all these celebrities," Kate was remarking in a hushed tone, drawing up shoulders barely covered by swaths of pink fabric, a color that complimented the summery tones of her blond hair and light eyes.

"I recognize that guy from TV," continued Sherry. "Isn't he on one of the afternoon soaps?"

"*All My Children*," returned Kate, trying not to stare.

"Who would have thought you'd see TV personalities in a Chinese restaurant?" asked Ed, trying his best not to look impressed, his eyes sliding to Trudy as if seeing her for the first time. "I admit it, I've never even heard of this place."

Truman shrugged. "It's an old New York haunt. They keep it out of the guidebooks. And it's fancy for Chinatown. Most places down here are mom-and-pop establishments."

"Didn't you need reservations?" asked Bob curiously, then glanced quickly away since everyone had been making studious efforts not to reference this morning when they'd made their plans.

"And without a reservation, they seated us at the most prominent table," Kate barreled on, clearly self-conscious since their table was on a platform, in front of a bay window, which allowed them to watch the throngs of shoppers on Canal Street.

Truman shrugged. "Well, the Pangs know Trudy, of course." When she kicked him under the table, he continued with the truth. "On top of that, years ago, my father was working as a beat cop. He got his start in Hell's Kitchen, but the year I was born, he got transferred to Chinatown because of his special interest in New York gangs."

"How fascinating," enthused Kate. "A gang specialist!"

Truman nodded. "One gang, the Dragons of Death, were extorting protection money from business owners on this street, and my father—his name's Augustus Steele—was a key player in chasing them out." Pausing, Truman pointed through the window. "But before that, he and Jen Pang got to be friends. Well, one night, Pop was dining at this table with Jen and his wife, and the Dragons of Death drove by, spraying bullets through this window—"

Sherry gasped, turning and staring through the window as if for the first time. "This window? This one right here?"

Truman nodded. "This very one. Pop yanked Jen's wife out of the line of fire and saved her life."

"The *News* reported the rescue," put in Trudy. "Truman's father was on the cover." She flashed him a smile. "Something I didn't realize until today."

Truman nodded. "Which got Pop another promotion."

Kate shook her head in astonishment. "No wonder we've had the royal treatment."

"And, like I said, the Pangs know Trudy," Truman reminded, once more ignoring the kick under the table. Glancing around, he suddenly felt glad to be here. He loved this place, and he didn't come often enough. As far back as he could recall, the Steeles had spent the Chinese New Year dining with the Pangs. Together, seated at this table, the two families jointly celebrated the fateful moment when their paths had crossed. Mary Pang had lived, Augustus's career had taken off, and without the Dragons of Death around, the Pangs' restaurant had thrived. Every year since birth, Truman had stared through this window, mesmerized by fireworks, sparklers and dancing dragons, as Chinatown went wild with the new year.

Now it seemed fitting to bring Trudy's family here. Not because they'd be wined and dined in the highest New York style, but because Truman associated Jen Pang's restaurant with the joining of two very different families whose lives were destined to become intertwined. He no longer had any doubt that the connection he'd made with Trudy was meant to last.

"And you're a patrolman?" asked Terrence Busey conversationally. He'd recovered from this morning's shock, and was assessing Truman with blue eyes astonishingly like his daughter's. Couldn't the man see it was Trudy, not his sons, who'd inherited his sharp eye and nose for news? "Yes, a family of cops?" Terrence mused thoughtfully.

Truman had already divulged the information, but Terrence was fishing for more. It wasn't the first time he'd probed. Truman was beginning to think the man wouldn't be satisfied until Truman submitted blood and urine samples. "Yes, sir." He shot Trudy an easy smile. "Trudy's met my family, of course." All evening, he'd been making it sound as if he and Trudy had been going out longer than they had since he didn't want the Buseys to think this was some fly-by-night affair. "They just love her," he added.

She kicked him again.

Bob looked at Ed. "We hadn't heard she was involved..."

Hearing the soft tinkle of Trudy's laughter, Truman fought not to laugh, himself. When she waved an airy hand, implying she had more lovers than a reasonable woman could keep track of, Kate and Sherry's lips parted in surprise. Their eyes flickered once more over their sister-in-law. "Well," murmured Trudy with nonchalance. "I don't think to mention *everything* when I come home for Christmas."

Sherry's chuckle was too high-pitched. "Don't you mean *everyone?*"

"I'd stick with this fellow," teased Kate, pointing toward Truman. "He's quite the catch."

To her credit, Trudy didn't gush, but merely shot

Truman a long, sideways glance, her eyes flicking down, over his dark suit. She smiled. "I suppose he'll do."

He did his best imitation of a sheepish chuckle. "You know Trudy," he said. "She keeps me hopping, not to mention half the cops in the NYPD."

Looking mortified, her father took a quick drink of water as if he were about to choke. "She dates other officers?"

Truman's lips parted in astonishment. Terrence Busey actually thought he'd been referencing Trudy's personal, not professional, life. Well, maybe this was what the man deserved for not giving Trudy her due. Truman sighed. He knew as well as anyone that when it came to family dynamics, it took years for changes to occur. No matter what he did, his older brothers still saw him as a kid, but tonight, he was going to make sure things started changing for Trudy. "The NYPD," he said. "All the cops love her, Terrence. Most out-of-town reporters play it all wrong." Truman shook his head in disgust. "You know how it is," he complained. "They go to some fancy school..."

He paused just long enough for Bob and Ed to contemplate their Ivy League educations. "Then they breeze into town," he continued. "Without bothering to get the lay of the land, they jump right in and start working crime beats."

"What's wrong with that?" asked Kate innocently.

"Without New York street experience, hotshot newcomers foul things up," Truman explained. "They're the bane of our existence. More than one hayseed journalist has ruined a case by printing too much, too soon."

Trudy chose just the right moment to break in. "Now, honey," she said. "Don't get yourself all worked up. There are lots of good reporters at the *New York News*."

"Better than at the *Times*," he muttered.

"Well, the *Times* is more international," she countered as if to placate him. "They can't be bothered with local politics."

"At least you're another breed." Truman glanced around, his gaze taking in all those at the table. "Of course, Trudy never toots her own horn. I bet she doesn't tell you half of what she does over at the *News*. More than anyone over there, she's aware of the cops. She knows the men, their families, their work..."

She kicked him a final time, but he ignored it. "Personally," he continued. "I think it's funny. Dimi Slovinsky—that's her boss—he's always trying to put her on the high-profile stuff, but Trudy's too busy winning the respect of people she'll need to rely on later in her career. She's built up an incredible list of sources. I know plenty of cops who'd go out on a limb to give her information." That much was true. Or it would be, once they heard Trudy was a friend of Truman's.

"So, you're eventually going to do high-profile stuff?" Kate asked Trudy, impressed. "We only see you when you come home. We had no idea."

"This *is* my home," corrected Trudy with a smile.

"New York City," said Sherry. "It's so exciting."

"No, honey," Bob interjected, barely able to contain his condescending tone as he addressed his wife. "No matter how many contacts she's got, Trudy can't go from doing stories about ice sculptures to hard crime."

"Be interesting to see who solves that Glass Slipper

case," added Ed, making Trudy even less the focal point. "And, uh," he added, "I saw those pictures at Trudy's place. Are you hoping to move up to working vice someday, Truman? Is that why she was taking pictures of you in front of those...uh, shops?"

Previously, her family had avoided referencing the pictures of Truman, but when the opportunity arose to passively jab at him, Ed couldn't resist, mostly because he couldn't tolerate the appreciative glances Kate and Sherry were sending Trudy's date.

"Actually," Truman returned, "I like patrol. Eventually, I'll wind up in gang-related crime, though. Vice doesn't interest me. Although I was in the Bryant Park-Times Square area, working on a vice-related crime," lowering his voice, he whispered so only Trudy could hear, "vice only interests me on a personal level."

"I see," Ed was saying. "You're following in your father's footsteps. That should make the climb up the ladder a lot easier for you."

Apparently Ed wasn't too quick on his toes. "Has that been your experience?" Truman volleyed innocently. "It's my understanding that you and Ed both work for your father?" He grinned easily. "Has that made for an easy climb for you?"

The silence was uncomfortable, but Truman didn't care. These people needed to start taking Trudy—and her friends—seriously. Before they could answer, he shot Trudy a warm glance. "Now here's a woman who's working her own way up."

"Well," put in Bob with a chuckle, clearly meaning to cut through the tension, but only making things worse. "Seeing as Trudy's got all those contacts on the

police force, maybe she'll be the one to break the Glass
Slipper story."

"Maybe she will."

That time, Terrence Busey had spoken.

It was a victory. Nevertheless, Truman was glad to
see Jen Pang wending through the crowd. Short in stat-
ure, the man was nearly seventy, but his body was
honed by the martial arts he practiced daily, and his
wrinkled face was wizened, each line etched by a life of
hard work.

"The Glass Slipper," Trudy repeated dreamily.
"Maybe I will break it." She laughed. "Not the slipper," she amended. "The story."

Truman's heart pulled. Trudy desperately wanted
her father to acknowledge her professional work, and
right now, he looked sorry he never had. Ed and Bob
cared for their sister as best as they knew how, but they
lacked her innate savvy, high energy and mental
sharpness. Deep down, the men knew it, so they tried
to make her look bad, to cover the fact that they ran a
newspaper that should have been hers. Not so, Terrence. He'd tried to keep his daughter out of the news
business to protect her, and now that he saw there was
no stopping her, he regretted the decision not to support her as his successor to the *Milton Herald*. He'd lost
his baby girl, just like his wife, to the big time.

"Hello!" Jen Pang reached the table. Setting down a
tip tray, he returned Ed's credit card. "Thank you, sir,"
said Jen, circling to stand behind Trudy and Truman.
"But you no pay." Glancing down with lively dark
eyes, Jen took in Trudy's family, then said exactly what
Truman had asked him to. "Trudy? She don't pay," he

assured. "She's our favorite reporter from the *New York News*."

A moment later, as they were rising to leave, Trudy leaned and whispered, "You made me look like a million bucks. I don't know how I can repay you. This was too terrific."

"Repayment?" Truman's gaze meshed with hers. "I can think of all kinds of ways. What say, I tell you when we get home?"

Home. He let the word linger as he took in her rose-tinged cheeks and beaming smile, hoping to impress upon her that they were starting to share a life. "Home," he repeated, momentarily forgetting why they were here, and that her family was present. For a moment, he even forgot the steamy fantasies he'd been having all night about removing that black dress. There was only her face.

Leaning, not caring who was watching, he brushed a tender kiss to her lips. It quickly heated, burning through his body as the pressure deepened. When her tongue flicked gently inside his mouth, desire stirred, and unstoppable warmth poured through his veins, melting the backs of his knees. A rumble of approval emanated from his chest as he tightened his hands around her back. Knowing he'd better stop before he couldn't, he thought. *Home.* They'd be there soon enough.

When he drew back, Truman heard one of Trudy's sisters-in-law, he wasn't sure which, whisper, "Wow."

Truman couldn't agree more.

9

"YOUR GIRLFRIEND AGAIN," Trudy teased the next day, still overjoyed by what had happened with her family, snagging a note from under a windshield wiper as she circled the cruiser. Balancing a steno pad under a latte from Starbucks, she got in the car, slammed the door while Truman did the same, then glanced at the busy corner of Broadway and Astor Place.

Setting his cup on the dashboard, Truman leaned in for a fast, deep kiss, then started the motor. "Go ahead. I know you're dying to read me her note." Letting the engine idle, he leaned his neck against the headrest, shooting Trudy an expectant look as he draped an arm along the back of the seat.

"Really," she protested playfully. "You know I don't have time to keep track of all your affairs. I need to—"

"Work. I know. But you've got to loosen up, Tru." Dropping his hand, he squeezed her shoulder, his eyes turning serious. "We deserve time together."

The emotion in her eyes deepened as she thought of his effect on her family last night. "You're right."

"Besides," he said, eyes twinkling. "It's Saturday."

"You're on duty," she reminded. Since she wasn't, she'd worn old jeans, a T-shirt and her gray, hooded sweatshirt jacket.

"The NYPD never sleeps." Laughing, he sipped his coffee. "I didn't last night, anyway."

"Somebody kept me awake," she seconded. "He cracked open a bottle of champagne he'd left chilling in the fridge, then lapped it from my navel."

"Hard to sleep through that," Truman commiserated.

Suppressing a rush of arousal, Trudy concentrated on Candy's note. "'Why aren't you calling me?'" Trudy read. She glanced up. "Candy's getting more aggressive. Maybe you ought to contact her and let her know you're not interested in a date."

He considered. "What if she takes it as encouragement?"

"Good point." Trudy continued reading. "'I was trying to be friendly, which is why I asked you to dinner, Officer Steele. I just don't get it. You were so nice to me when you arrested me that I thought you might be the right cop to approach, but if you don't call me today, I'm going to somebody else at your precinct.'" Trudy frowned, studying Candy's signature a long moment. "It sounds as if she's got some sort of lead, Truman."

Reaching, he took the note and quickly reread it. "Or this is a ploy to have dinner with me."

Trudy wasn't so sure. "You're cute," she admitted. "I, more than anyone, can see why a woman would want a date."

He grinned. "Thanks."

"However..." Trudy shook her head. "My sixth sense says Candy's feeling you out about something. You treated her nicely, so she's approaching you with information. Candy," she mused on the name. "Short for Candice?"

"Candice Dicappicio."

"Italian?"

"Dicappicio?" Truman returned with irony. "Is that really a question, Trudy?" She smirked playfully, and Truman continued, "She lives with her great-aunt Christina on Mulberry Street in Little Italy. I arrested her there on a domestic-violence call. She's got a re-straining order against an ex-husband who's trying to win her back—name of Dino. Anyway, one day when Candy'd had a little too much wine, Dino showed up, broke down the door and entered the home. She bashed him with a pot."

"A pot?"

He nodded. "Dutch oven full of spaghetti sauce. You should have seen the place. It was a mess. Red sauce was everywhere."

"Good for her." Trudy nodded approvingly, then stared thoughtfully through the windshield at a side-walk crowded with Saturday shoppers. She took in the Starbucks, Astor Liquor, a Barnes and Noble and a hair salon that also offered body piercing. Her eyes settled on some workers standing outside the smudged glass door to their union building. A sign on the glass said Local Number 784.

"I love this city," she suddenly said, smiling.

"Me, too."

"I love that we have that in common."

"Me, too."

She took in the corner of Astor Place and Broadway where the relatively staid West Village ended, giving way to the unruly East, wondering if she and Truman would wind up staying together, and trying to ignore the worry that came with relying on someone. She took in St. Marks Place, across Broadway, which was lined with Indian restaurants, newspaper vendors and kiosks of silver jewelry and leather goods. "Maybe Candy knows something about your family's contributions on the force," Trudy commented, pulling her mind back to business. "I mean, maybe she knows you've got an interest in gangs."

"You're thinking she knows something about the mob?"

She shrugged, studying Truman a long moment, and marveling over finding him. How many woman knew men who met their needs, both sexually and intellectually? "She sounds like a tough cookie."

He considered. "She is, and she's not."

"Now, there's clear cop thinking," teased Trudy.

"Candy's a good Catholic girl," Truman explained. "She goes to mass every morning, never misses a day. When I arrested her, she cried her eyes out. She said divorce was a sin, and because she left Dino, she deserves to be punished. She feels guilty about getting a restraining order against him because he's her husband, even though the guy won't leave her alone. Anyway, she'd been doing work for the altar guild at St. Carmine's when she got a stressful phone—"

"Call from Dino?" Trudy supplied.

Truman nodded, rolling down his window and dragging a hand through long, light brown strands of hair before taking another sip of coffee. "Let's just say it was the wrong time for Candy to be around all that holy wine."

Trudy's eyes widened. "She drank the church's wine?"

"She swore the priest hadn't blessed it yet," returned Truman with a soft chuckle. "But after the upsetting call from Dino, she sat down in the choir room, had a good cry and a few too many glasses of free Burgundy, then she took a cab home."

"Which is when Dino showed up at her great-aunt Christina's apartment, where she'd been staying since she left him?"

"Exactly."

Trudy shook her head, smiling. "What a mess."

Gingerly removing the lid of the coffee cup, Truman blew across the top and took another sip. "Despite the restraining order, Candy couldn't bring herself to press charges against Dino, so he didn't charge her with assault. I talked to both of them awhile, then they shook hands and went home."

Trudy bit back a smile. "So, you did a little marriage counseling?"

"Divorce counseling was more like it."

Trudy's heart swelled as she thought of how Truman had treated her when she'd told him about her mother's abandonment. He'd offered just the right mix of concern and humor. "I bet you were good."

His eyebrows knitted. "What? At talking to them?"

"Yeah." Trudy blew out a sigh, her emotions humbling. She and Truman were so physically compatible. Could that overcome her fears? Her impulse to bolt? Suddenly, she frowned, her gaze settling on the union building. *Local Number 784.* The workers had filed inside, except for one woman who'd remained on the sidewalk. Trudy was sure she'd been staring at the cruiser, too. She was tall. Slender but full-bodied, with curly jet hair that cascaded over her shoulders, and she was wearing a blue ribbed top with a knee-length blue skirt. A designer shoebox was tucked under her arm. Seeing that, Trudy's eyes lowered to the woman's shoes. Nearly spilling her coffee, Trudy grabbed Truman's arm. On a hunch, she said, "How old's Candy?"

"Twenty-five." He rattled off her birth date, adding, "Funny what a cop's mind retains, isn't it?"

"Look," Trudy whispered, choosing to ignore Truman's reference to his own intelligence at the moment. "Look at that woman, Tru."

He followed her gaze. "Speak of the devil. That's Candy. I guess we ought to go find out about this hot tip, huh?"

Trudy's eyes were still riveted on her feet. "No," she persisted. "Look at the shoes."

Truman's gaze dropped. "What are they made of? Glass?"

From this distance, Trudy couldn't tell if they were designer originals or knockoffs. "Most likely high-grade plastic," she returned, her eyes studying the iridescent high heels that turned pink, purple, or blue, depending on the light. "But they look like glass. I've seen them before." Trudy's heart pounded. But where? She wracked her brain. "The Sundance Film Festival," she finally said slowly. "I might be wrong, though. And I don't remember who wore them." Names of actresses filtered through her mind: Helen Hunt? Jodie Foster? Geena Davis?

Truman's eyes pierced the windshield. "Are you sure?"

"I could be wrong, but I...I think Candy's been watching us the whole time." Now she was standing on the curb in front of the union building, looking the other way, as if oblivious to them. A large moving van passed between them, and Trudy held her breath, half expecting Candy to be gone once the van passed, but she was still there. "Maybe she doesn't want to approach you while I'm in the car," Trudy guessed. "For all we know, she's been following you for the past two weeks, trying to talk to you."

Turning off the ignition, Truman pocketed the keys, his hand closing over the door handle. "Let's go see what she wants."

Getting out in tandem with Truman, Trudy realized the coffee cup was still in her hand and quickly set it on the roof of the car. Truman tossed his into an overflowing trash can before jaywalking across the street, wending between cars that were nearly bumper-to-bumper. Candy hadn't yet noticed them. Trudy's heartbeat accelerated as she followed Truman.

Suddenly Candy turned around. Her eyes widened as she registered their approach, then she edged backward, tucking the shoebox more firmly under her arm and glancing nervously over her shoulder toward the door of the union building.

Don't run, Trudy silently begged, excitement tunneling through her, adrenaline racing in her veins. *Stay there.* What if her hunch was right? What if the shoes Candy wore belonged to a famous actress and Trudy was about to break the Glass Slipper story?

"Candy?" Truman shouted over the traffic sounds, sensing she was about to bolt. "I know you've been trying to contact me. Sorry I didn't respond. We need to talk."

"Who's that with you?" Candy called.

"A friend," he returned. "A reporter from the *News.*"

Whirling abruptly, Candy bolted from the curb, nearly mowing down a businessman who'd just come from Starbucks. He spun to keep his balance, coffee in one hand, briefcase in the other. Trudy rushed forward, sidestepping him, running behind Truman as Candy pushed through the glass door of the union building, moving so fast that her long, black curls flew wildly over her shoulders. She darted toward a flight of stairs, but before the door swung shut, Truman's palms flattened on the glass. He shoved, and Trudy lunged inside behind him, just in time to see him grab the back of Candy's shirt. "Hold it right there, Candy."

"Where did those shoes come from?" Trudy demanded breathlessly, pointing down. "And what's in the shoebox?"

With two nervous jerks of her head, Candy sent her hair over her shoulder. "You've got to be quiet," she warned in a hushed voice. "We can't talk here. Somebody might hear us."

Trudy stared. "You don't want somebody at the union to hear you talk about your shoes?"

"That's what I said," Candy returned darkly. Further lowering her voice, she whispered, "I think somebody wore these at the Oscars. Maybe the Golden Globe Awards. Or the Sundance Festival." She gasped. "Some cop," she added venomously as Truman took a well-worn card from his pocket and began reading her Miranda rights. When he handed the shoebox to Trudy, so he could hook handcuffs around Candy's wrists, Candy said, "I'm trying to help you, Officer Steele."

"When we get to Manhattan South," assured Truman, "you can give your statement."

"These are just old sandals," Trudy said, unable to

mask her disappointment as she peeked inside the shoebox. "The strap's broken."

"I was taking them to the shoe shop." Candy glared between Trudy and Truman as they left the union building and threaded through heavy traffic again. "And for what we pay in city taxes," Candy huffed, "you'd think officers could return phone calls, instead of chatting up girls in their patrol cars all day."

Looking confused as he urged Candy into the back seat of the cruiser, Truman said, "Chatting up girls?"

Candy stared at Trudy. "It's all you've been doing for the past two weeks. I know," she added, "because I've been following you two."

"YOU CAN'T ARREST ME," Candy protested moments later, as Truman cut through the West Village and pulled into a line of taxis on Sixth Avenue, heading uptown.

He glanced over his shoulder, through the wiremesh partition between the seats. "We need to know where you got those shoes."

"Where are you taking me?"

"I told you," he repeated. "The precinct. Manhattan South."

"And I told you," Candy returned, now sounding panicked, "Someone wore these shoes to the Oscars or the Sundance Festival, I don't remember which."

"How did the shoes come into your hands?" Trudy asked, preparing to rapidly fire questions, a tactic calculated to fluster a person into telling the truth. Turning in the seat, she balanced the steno pad on her knee as she scribbled her impressions about Candy. "Who did the shoes belong to? Why are you so hesitant to talk? You've been trying to contact Officer Steele for days. Why, when he found you, did you run?"

"Because you were with him," Candy said, her voice tense, her eyes darting around the cruiser. "And maybe I realized he was going to arrest me. I didn't do anything wrong, though. Neither did my great-aunt Christina. That's why I—" Candy scooted forward on the back seat. Bringing her handcuffed hands to the wire screen, she twined her fingers through the mesh and stared at Truman imploringly. "You didn't call me back," she continued, her voice restrained as if by sheer force of will.

Truman glanced at her in the rearview mirror. "I thought you wanted to go on a date," he admitted calmly. "I didn't realize you were calling for other reasons."

"What are those reasons?" Trudy asked quickly. "What's your great-aunt Christina got to do with this?"

Candy's dark eyes were turning glassy with unshed tears, and her expression was a strange mix of righteous indignation and hot, suppressed fury. For a second, she muttered in lethal-sounding Italian, then she focused her rage on Trudy, staring murderously in her direction.

"Men," she said simply, her voice low.

"Men?" prompted Trudy, wondering how she could get Candy to talk. Pushing too hard would be a mistake, but this woman held the key to unlocking the Glass Slipper case. She gentled her voice. "Men?" she repeated. "Have you been wronged by men?"

Lifting her chin a prideful notch, Candy nodded toward Truman. "When he talked to me and Dino, he seemed so nice and reasonable." Slowly, she shook her head. Her eyes, now wounded, took in the view of Sixth Avenue as if she couldn't believe any of this was happening. "You thought I wanted a *date?*" she suddenly repeated on a groan. Adamantly, she shook her head, adding, "Oh, no. No more men." She pierced Trudy with a glare. "Did he tell you about my ex?"

"Yes, how horrible," Trudy commiserated quickly. "Dino sounds like a..." She searched for a word, then emphatically settled on, "*monster.*"

"And what kind of woman does *he* think I am?" Candy railed, pointing at Truman with her cuffed hands. "He thinks I wanted a date? Ha! Another man?" She shook her head again. "Not on your life!"

Trudy listened patiently as Candy plunged into the saga of her relationship with Dino: how they'd grown up together, meeting in parochial school, but how she'd finally figured out he was cheating on her. As she spoke, Trudy's eyes locked on Truman's, the silent communication passing between them unlike anything she'd ever felt. Without saying a word, they'd fallen into perfect good cop, bad cop roles, and Candy was reacting to Trudy's sympathy.

"I'm sorry," Trudy murmured, her heart going out to the younger woman. "Not all men cheat."

Candy stared at Truman for long moments, then at Trudy. "You keep telling yourself that, lady."

A lump lodged in her throat, and Trudy worked to swallow around it, since without her even realizing it, Truman was starting to convince her not to expect betrayals. As she listened to Candy describe how she'd subdued Dino by attacking him with the pot of spaghetti sauce, Trudy hoped Candy got beyond her experience someday. It would be a shame for such a passionate young woman to shut herself off from love.

"The wine for communion," she was saying now. "I can't believe I drank it. I'm not a bad person. If my sandals hadn't broken, I wouldn't be wearing these stolen shoes, but when the strap gave, I had no other choice. Anyway, the wine wasn't blessed, thank God, and I was all alone at the church, and Dino wouldn't leave me alone, and..."

"It's understandable," assured Trudy.

Getting tired of waiting for information, Truman decided to play bad cop again. "C'mon. Why were you tracking me down?"

"It's about the shoes, Officer Steele. I didn't steal the ones I'm wearing," Candy added defensively. "But I know who did, and I'll talk if she gets immunity from prosecution."

Trudy's pulse quickened. She lived for moments such as this. She and Truman were seconds from breaking a story. Because Gracie Dale from the lottery board was also considering talking, Trudy might break the lottery story this week, as well. She'd love to find out who'd won the fifteen million dollars. "One?" Trudy hammered out. "Are you saying more than one person is involved in the thefts of these shoes?"

"Of course more than one person is involved," Candy said incredulously. "Did you really think only one person stole a thousand pairs of shoes?"

"It's an investigation," Truman said. "We don't assume anything, Candy. We ask questions."

"A thousand?" echoed Trudy. "Only about a hundred pairs have been reported missing."

"Well," said Candy importantly. "There's more.

Lots more." Realizing they were approaching the station, she added, "But I want immunity. Not just for me, but for one other person. Since I knew about this, I'm an accomplice." Her voice suddenly shook. "The woman I'm trying to protect is almost sixty-four, and she's got arthritis and osteoporosis. Honestly, she didn't realize she could go to jail. When so many people agreed to steal the shoes..."

"She who?" Trudy coaxed.

"My great-aunt Christina," confessed Candy, her black eyebrows knitting in concern. "When I left Dino, she was nice enough to take me in. She still works, but she needs help at home, cleaning, doing laundry, getting groceries—"

"How's this connected to the shoes?" asked Trudy.

Candy considered. "I have to cut a deal first."

"Immunity," said Truman promptly. "No problem."

Trudy sent him a level look. Truman needed senior input before he could grant such a thing. "You say your aunt stole only one of the pairs of shoes?" Trudy continued.

"Great-aunt," corrected Candy. "She took the ones I'm wearing. She works for Manhattan Maids."

"I've seen the vans they use to transport workers," Trudy said to Truman, who nodded affirmation.

"Her arthritis is so bad that it's hard for her to clean apartments," Candy continued, "but she has to, to pay the rent. Anyway, when the mayor started closing all the mental health facilities, putting all those people on the street..." She sighed. "Well, you can imagine how great-aunt Christina felt, since she's always so worried about her own situation."

Trudy's gaze meshed with Truman's once more. What could the closing of mental health facilities have to do with stolen shoes? Nothing was making sense.

"Don't get me wrong," Candy corrected quickly. "My great-aunt Christina isn't the mastermind."

"Of course not," demurred Trudy. "But could you describe her involvement?"

Candy took a deep breath, seemingly willing herself to go on. "When an unnamed party suggested that Manhattan Maids and all the other workers in the domestic union—"

"The domestic workers' union?" repeated Trudy, scribbling happily in her pad, since things were starting to fall into place. Just moments ago, she and Truman had been parked on Astor Place, right across from the building. "That's local 784?"

"Right," said Candy, looking relieved. "Someone from C.L.A.S.P.—that's the City and Local Activists for Street People—brought flyers to great-aunt Christina's union, asking for clothing donations for the homeless."

Truman shook his head in disbelief. "A lady with long gray hair?" he guessed, realizing it was his mother. "She wears it in a bun? She's in her mid-fifties?"

"Yes," continued Candy. "Everyone wanted to help, as you can imagine..." She shook her head sadly. "But a lot of domestic workers, like great-aunt Christina, don't have extra clothes to spare. So, since Manhattan Maids work in upscale neighborhoods, the maids decided to ask their clients for contributions while they were cleaning their apartments. They figured all these rich women would be glad to put together a bag of old clothes..."

Candy's lips turned downward. "Well, you'll never believe this," she continued, "but they refused. Once, when great-aunt Christina asked for a donation, the woman whose house she was cleaning said Aunt Christina just wanted some free fancy clothes for herself." Candy gasped. "Can you imagine?"

"Pretty heartless," agreed Trudy, catching Truman's eye.

"And others met with the same response?" prodded Truman.

Candy nodded. "Oh, we got some donations, but not many..."

"And so everyone decided to steal a token," guessed Trudy. "To steal from the rich and give to the poor. Just like Robin Hood. And the shoes were a one-of-a-kind thing. Something the women paid a hefty price for, but would never miss or wear again."

"Exactly," said Candy. "I told Aunt Christina I'd drop these off for her at the new C.L.A.S.P. shelter for women in the meat-packing district, and I was on my way there when the strap on my sandals broke, so I put these on."

"Wow," said Truman, impressed. He glanced over his shoulder. "If all that's true," he assured, "I'll do what I can to help out, Candy. But stealing's stealing. You know what I mean?"

Candy nodded. "I'm so sorry, Officer Steele."

Trudy sighed, shaking her head as her mind scrolled down the list of actresses, politicians and models whose shoes were missing. When it got out that they hadn't been willing to help people in need, they'd never live it down. Suddenly, Trudy chuckled. "If the *News* prints this, the actresses are going to have to get involved in a cause." It was the only way the women would redeem themselves in the public eye.

"Looks like it," agreed Truman.

As soon as he pulled into the precinct garage, Trudy hopped out of the cruiser, propelled by her excitement. She'd gotten pages of material from Candy, and now she needed to get to the *News*, tell Dimi she'd broken the story and write it before somebody, namely Scott Smith-Sanker, scooped her. Time was precious. "The homeless women," she suddenly whispered, stopping in her tracks and staring at Truman, who'd circled the car.

He halted in front of her. Gazing down, he smiled warmly into her eyes. "Yep," he agreed. "This is a great story, Busey. A career-maker."

She shook her head, willing him to understand. "No. I'm talking about the photographs at my apartment!" Flinging her arms around his neck, she hugged him more tightly than she'd ever hugged anyone, breathing deeply and pulling his arousing scent all the way into her lungs. When her eyes found his again, she breathlessly continued, "I've got to get to my place! You take Candy's formal statement and try to get Coombs to grant her immunity. Surely he won't jail a bunch of old maids—"

Cutting herself off, Trudy flung her head back, laughing in glee while Truman wrapped his arms around her back. "Old Maids," she said happily. "Maybe I can work that into the title. I mean, we thought the culprit was Prince Charming—only to find it was a bunch of old maids! Remember the card game?" Before Truman could answer, she raced on passionately. "Can't you just see it on the cover of the *News?*"

He was peering at her, his eyes alive with the same excitement she was feeling. "What about the photographs?"

"I knew there was something strange about the ones I took of you near Bryant Park," she explained quickly. "I keep staring at them, unable to figure out what's wrong." She'd been so busy focusing on Truman that she'd barely noticed the people around him, and when she'd photographed the homeless, she'd taken close-ups, attending to their faces. Nuzzling Truman's chest, she laughed again. "The homeless women in Bryant Park," she said with a smile. "They're wearing the missing shoes."

Truman's jaw dropped. "No joke? You've got evidence?"

"Pictures to me," she corrected. "Evidence to you." She nodded happily. "More pairs have been stolen than were ever reported." She simply couldn't believe it. "These are one-of-a-kind items, Truman. Women put them in boxes and never take them out again. Whoever owns the shoes Candy's wearing hasn't even missed them yet."

Grinning, he spanked her on the butt. "Get going, Busey. We can't have that jerk, Scott, scooping you on this story. I'll keep a lid on it as long as possible, and I'll try to get Coombs to do the same, so none of the other cops will call their favorite reporters, but you'll have to hurry."

She beamed at him, barely aware that Candy, still in the car, was getting restless. "You mean I'm not the only reporter in town who's sleeping with her main source?''

"I knew it," Truman teased. "All along, you've only been seducing me for information."

"Better than for your money," she shot back.

He looked at her a long moment, the expression odd, as if there were something on the tip of his tongue he desperately wanted to tell her, but before she could ask him what, he said, "Here. You might need this." Angling his head down, he engaged her lips in a wet, decidedly sloppy kiss, then he drew away and reached, lifting her coffee cup from the roof of the car. He handed it to her.

"It stayed on the roof?" she asked, laughing again, now in astonishment. "I put it up there when we chased Candy," she said, amazed that it had made the trip all the way from Astor Place to Manhattan South.

"It's a good omen," said Truman.

"Definitely," she agreed. Gripping the coffee and her steno pad, she squeezed her arms around his waist once more. She'd never felt so happy. She'd remember this moment forever. Even as they stood there, clinging to each other, she was tucking away the memory, pasting it into the scrapbook of her mind. "We did it," she whispered. Together. As a team. And then she added words she never thought she'd hear herself speak. "I love you, Truman. I really do."

"I'm a cop," he returned, pressing kisses into her hair. "So, I was starting to suspect that."

"Tonight," she promised, "I'll give you evidence."

"I'll have hard evidence, myself," he assured. "I do hope yours is silk and slinky."

"It is," she said. But there was no time to savor their

personal and professional victory. He gave her one more quick kiss, and then she ran toward the street, raising her arm to hail a taxi. If the pictures she'd taken in Bryant Park showed what she thought, she and Truman were about to share the story—and case—of the year.

"Not a Pulitzer," she whispered as a taxi screeched to a halt. "But this is close."

10

"HURRY," TRUDY WHISPERED, her fingers shaking as she turned keys in the numerous locks on her apartment door. Pushing inside, she crossed the room, nearly toppling the chair around which Truman had slung the suit jacket he'd worn to dinner the previous night. Righting it, she headed for the photos hanging from the clothesline she'd strung across the room.

"I knew it." She trailed a finger down a dark, grainy picture. Standing under the marquee of an X-rated movie, Truman looked every inch the degenerate, but in the corner, almost outside the camera frame, a woman draped in dark tattered clothes was sitting on the curb. Her clothes were bulky, too heavy for the season, and only when Trudy squinted could she make out platform sneakers.

If she'd had any remaining doubt that this was what she'd find, it had been dispelled on the taxi ride home. Perched on the seat, mentally willing the cab to go faster, Trudy had stared in wonder through the window. New York crowds swarmed the sidewalks, the people swept along by the pace of the city, their eyes intent on destinations, no one registering the strange sight all around them. Nobody glanced toward the dispossessed, the ragged people in ragged clothes who watched the world go by from street curbs and subway grates.

"There!" Trudy snagged a photo. "That's tomorrow's front page." A businessman was rushing out of Grand Central Station, carrying a briefcase and the *News*, the cover of which depicted a close-up of a missing boat-style shoe. On the curb in front of the harried executive, right under his nose, sat two women—one sporting spangled slippers, the other showcasing sequined mules.

"This is what they call a paradigm shift." Trudy was seeing everything in a new light, as if her eyes had been opened for the first time. It reminded her of an old picture she'd often seen where, if you looked at it one way, it was two lamps, but seen from another perspective, the lamps appeared to be two faces. The world, she thought, taking in the photo, is never as we assume. "Love, either," she whispered, her heart swelling. She'd built her emotional foundation on a faulty premise, just as Truman had initially built this case on the wrongful assumption that the perpetrator was a foot fetishist. Years ago, Trudy's mother had left, simply slipped into her clothes the day Trudy was born and left the hospital, but it didn't mean Trudy wasn't lovable. Truman had shown her that. How had she come so dangerously close to not seeing how wonderful he was? To realizing a world of riches was right here, waiting to come into their lives? She shook her head as if to clear it. It was amazing how love had come when she'd least expected it, sweeping into her life and changing her perspective...

"I need the negatives," she murmured, pulling her mind back to work even though her throat had tightened with emotion. She was only an amateur shutterbug, but the guys in the *News*'s darkroom would lighten the photographs, making the shoes more visible.

She'd almost finished gathering the negatives when the cell phone rang. She started not to answer it. But what if it was Truman? Or Dimi? Wincing, she hoped Dimi was at the office. He usually worked on Saturday. "So does Scott," she muttered. Taking the phone from her handbag, she lifted it. "Hello?"

"Hello," her father said. "I didn't catch you on the machine, so I thought I'd try the cell. We were hoping to see you again before we leave town. Your boyfriend, too." He paused. "I like him, Trudy."

In her excitement, she'd forgotten her family was still here. "Dad," she managed, her heart clenching when she registered his approval. She glanced around for something to put the negatives and photos in. "I'm sorry," she continued. "I can't talk right now. The Glass Slipper story's breaking. I'll call you at your hotel if I can."

"The story?" Terrence Busey's voice sharpened, gaining the edge she'd loved hearing when she was a kid when he'd gotten a call at home about a story. Despite her need to get to the *News*, she felt her heart tug. Years dropped away, and she was eight years old again, realizing that other people sometimes needed her daddy more than she did. "You're breaking it, Trudy?"

She was still reacting to the supercharged intensity of his voice. "Yeah, I think—"

"You work for a national. This isn't the *Milton Herald*. You can't afford to think, you have to know. Are your facts straight?"

Had her father really compared the papers they

worked for, with his coming up short? Unwanted tears blurred her vision, and she covered the phone's mouthpiece, so he wouldn't hear her sudden sob of breath. For that second, the excitement of the moment—of the story, of sharing herself with Truman, of gaining her father's respect—was simply too much. "I've got the facts," she managed. "An interview. Pictures."

"Do the cops know who stole the shoes?"

He was questioning her as he did the reporters he most respected. "Yes. Truman's keeping a lid on it as long as he can. I'm supposed to call him when I get to the *News,* as soon as I get Dimi's approval to start writing."

"What are you doing in your apartment?" roared her father. "Hurry! And remember, whatever happens today, news is in your blood. Now move. This is one hot story. Everybody out there wants it. Don't let yourself get scooped."

Her heart lurched. "I won't, Daddy. This is mine."

The second before the word slipped out, she realized she hadn't called him *Daddy* in years. There was the slightest hesitation, then he roared, "Damn right you won't. You're my daughter."

Hanging up, she swiped at her eyes as she shoved photos and negatives into a plastic shopping bag printed with the I Love New York logo. Thrusting her hand through the bag's handle, she rushed for the door. In midstride, she toppled the chair again, and just as she righted it, an envelope fell from Truman's jacket. Snatching it, she reached to replace it, then froze, her eyes catching the words: *To Felix Kress/Confidential.*

"Felix Kress," she said, her body freezing, her eyes darting toward the door. She had to keep moving or Scott would scoop her, but Felix Kress was Gracie Dale's boss at the lottery board! And Gracie was the assistant who'd been considering divulging the identity of the lottery winner! That story was almost as big as the Glass Slipper. Everybody in New York wanted to know who'd won the fifteen million dollars. The envelope was addressed to the board, and the return address was Truman's.

The envelope was unsealed, too. Trudy couldn't stop herself from removing and rifling through the enclosures—forms asking for information from the lottery winner, which Truman had filled out. He'd won the fifteen million dollar jackpot? Her heart pounding, her eyes quickly returned to the top sheet, a chatty note from Sheila.

Dear Truman,

I don't know why the board sent this here. I gave them your address, and your brothers' forms seemed to have gone to their mailboxes. At least those didn't come here. Anyway, I decided to take this last opportunity to remind you that if you and your brothers don't find wives within the next three months, none of you are going to get this money. And don't forget, you can't tell the women that millions of dollars are at stake when you marry them! I'm the one who won, after all. So, I make the rules. You love me, so you know I'm not heartless. I can't stand to see you boys living alone anymore. Well, I hope you're starting to hear wedding bells...

Feeling sick, Trudy stared at the smiley face Sheila had drawn beneath her signature. Sure she must have misunderstood, she slowly reread the letter. "I can't believe this," she whispered. She'd realized Sheila was a little eccentric, but had she really won the lotto, then told her sons she'd divide the money between them if they found brides? "And not to tell the women that the marriage would bring the men a fortune?"

Was that why Truman had taken such an interest in her? Shock gave way to panic and pain as she tossed the envelope into the shopping bag with the photos and darted for the door. A second after she locked it behind her, she hit the steps at a run. She was thinking back to having lunch at the Steeles'. Sheila had urged her to pursue the lottery story, and now her voice was in Trudy's ears. *Maybe some poor, hopeless mother like me has got a bunch of grown bachelors for sons, and when she won, she said she wouldn't split the money between them until they got married.* Yes, Sheila had joked about the horrible thing she'd done, knowing she'd offered Truman a fortune to pursue a romantic interest. How could Truman have allowed his mother to use Trudy like that, as the butt of a joke?

Pain knifed through her heart as her feet connected with the sidewalk. Had Truman lied about his feelings? "Yes," she whispered. She was sure of it. Why else would a man who'd stayed out of committed relationships for ten years suddenly start proposing at every turn? She'd be a fool to think he wouldn't do so for his share of a fifteen-million-dollar lottery jackpot. She raised her voice, shouting, "Taxi!" As one pulled to the curb, Trudy muttered, "If I don't get to the *News,* Scott's going to break this story."

But she had to know if Truman loved her.

The cabbie growled, "Where are you going, lady?"

She gave the Steeles' address.

A MOMENT AGO, HIS HEART had been racing, his adrenaline pumping, and joy had been dancing in Truman's veins. When he'd seen the pleasure in Trudy's face as she'd kissed him goodbye in the parking garage, he'd known she belonged to him completely. Whatever sliver of self she'd been withholding was now his, and he'd do everything he could to keep that smile on her lips.

Including getting rid of Capote and Dern. Truman glanced through the glass door of his office. Across the squad room, Capote and Dern, the two cops to whom he'd supposedly handed the Glass Slipper case, were talking to Coombs. Biting back a soft curse at the thought that something might get in the way of Trudy's happiness, Truman resumed taking Candy's statement. "And the shoes you're wearing," he asked, as he began typing on the computer again, "they were taken from a residence at 3478 Park Avenue?"

"Correct," returned Candy. "Apartment 10."

"Which is the penthouse?"

"Yes."

Lifting his fingers from the keys, Truman stared toward his boss's office again. Coombs was sharp as a tack, but he was also the kind of guy who had to be in the know. Between that, and the grins on Capote's and Dern's faces, it was clear that Coombs was doing what he'd promised not to—discussing the Glass Slipper case. That meant that Capote and Dern would be heading to their phones any second now to call their favorite reporters. Where was Trudy? She'd sworn she'd call here as soon as she got to the *News*.

"Sorry," he murmured, hoping she was at the paper, and grabbing a cell phone. He punched in Trudy's number. Again.

No answer. He shook his head. "Why isn't she at the *News?*"

"Maybe her taxi wrecked," Candy said helpfully. "Or if she took the subway, maybe the electricity on the rails went out. You know how slow the trains can be on weekends."

Truman sighed. "Is that supposed to be encouraging?"

Candy winced. "Sorry."

Capote and Dern were exiting Coombs's office now, clapping each other on the back and heading for their phones. One of them would call the *News*. "Dammit," Truman cursed softly. "Where are you, Trudy?"

He was used to action. To 911 calls, police dispatches, and sirens that allowed him to cut through traffic, so he felt particularly helpless. Still, he had no choice but to wait. Vaguely, he was aware of the loud tick of a wall clock. Seconds seemed to last for minutes, and minutes for hours.

Didn't Trudy know she was about to lose the story of her career?

"C'MON. ANSWER THE DOOR." Trudy shifted her weight anxiously from one foot to the other, glancing from the Steeles' front stoop, all the way down their brownstone-lined street, feeling as if she'd lost her mind. She'd just walked out on her career-making story! She'd gone to the Steeles', instead of the *News*, caring more about Truman than the story, hoping against hope Sheila would tell her there was some mistake. No woman would, in effect, pay her sons to get married, would she? "But you read the letter," Trudy whispered, wondering if Sheila was doing charity work at C.L.A.S.P., but recalling that, during lunch, she'd said she stayed home on weekend days.

Clutching the shopping bag of photographs, Trudy settled her gaze on the cabbie who'd grudgingly agreed to keep the car running. He wasn't very happy about it. "Five minutes, lady," he'd barked meanly.

The bag in her hand was heavy, but she couldn't leave it in the seat of the taxi, for fear the man might change his mind and take off. Leaning, she repeatedly pressed the buzzer, putting her whole weight behind it. Was Sheila taking a walk? Keeping her eyes peeled, Trudy looked east, toward the kids playing in Abingdon Square Park, then west, toward the choppy Hudson River.

Just as she was about to ring again, Sheila swung open the door. She looked terrified—her hair wet, a plaid flannel robe clutched to her throat. In a heartbeat, Trudy realized that Sheila was related to four men who, on any given day, might be killed in the line of duty. Sheila pressed a hand to her heart. "Is everything all right?"

"Truman's fine," Trudy said quickly. *Just dishonest.* "I have a few questions for you."

"Come inside and sit down," Sheila said, then stared curiously toward the running cab. "I'm sorry I'm not dressed, I just got a call from Police Plaza, something about my husband, and I was rushing downtown—"

"I don't have time to sit," Trudy said shortly. She

could feel anger heating her body, touching her face and deepening its color. She hated the Steeles right now for putting her in this position. She was going to lose the Glass Slipper story because she'd rushed here instead of to the office, but she had to know the truth. She never should have let down her guard. Feelings she usually kept deeply buried kept trying to surface. Maybe, said a little voice inside her, Truman had known she was no good, just as her mother had. When he had to find a quick, throwaway wife, in order to get his hands on the lottery money, he'd known Trudy was the perfect pansy.

She held up the letter from the lottery board, and the one Sheila had written to Truman. "I need an explanation."

"Really," said Sheila, looking worried as she eyed the lottery board correspondence. "You'd better come in."

"I'm on a story," Trudy returned, hating how her voice shook with barely contained fury and pain. "And if I lose *that* one because I stopped here to chase down *this* one, I'll never forgive myself." Not to mention never forgive this eccentric woman and her lying son.

Sheila's eyes narrowed. "I thought you cared about my son?"

"I thought your son cared about me." *This lottery thing's just a story,* she told herself silently, trying not to panic. *You're following a lead, like any other lead.* "But it looks like there was a lot at stake in his affection." She paused. "Fifteen million dollars, to be exact."

"My sons have never shown much interest in settling down," Sheila explained quickly. "Augustus and I have been so happy, and I want them to find the kind of love we share. It's my fault they haven't. I've been too easy on them. They left home years ago, but I still feed them, do their laundry and darn their socks. Now I'm doing my best to push them from the nest."

"No matter who you hurt in the process?" Before Sheila could answer, Trudy's phone rang. Cursing softly and never taking her eyes from Sheila, she reached into her shoulder bag and turned it off, trying to ignore a flash fantasy of Scott reaching for his phone, then salivating as he listened to a hot tip about the Glass Slipper story.

"The last thing I wanted to do is hurt people," defended Sheila. "But when I won the lotto, I thought about all that money. Fifteen million. It was my big chance. I told the boys I'd divide it between them, but only on three conditions. Otherwise, I'd give the money to the Research Station on the Galapagos Islands."

She'd known the islands were Sheila's pet cause, and now Trudy's breath caught. Was it possible? "So the Galapagos oil spill, the lottery, and the Glass Slipper stories are all connected?"

"That's all this is to you?" Sheila gasped. "A story? What about my son?"

"Your son was using me."

"I don't believe that."

Trudy's lips parted in astonishment. Was this woman really going to deny her part in this? Steeling herself against emotion, Trudy nodded toward the letter in her hand. "I see only two conditions. All three of your sons need to find wives within three months, and they're not allowed to tell the woman a fortune hinges on her acceptance of a proposal." Trudy's eyes narrowed, and she tried not to think of how often Truman had raised the subject of marriage. "The third?"

"It has to be a love match. No marrying just to get their hands on the money."

Pain sliced through Trudy. That was the last thing she'd expected.

"You see," said Sheila. "He loves you."

"You don't think your son would lie for fifteen million dollars?"

Sheila looked mortally offended. "No."

The words were more revealing than Trudy intended. "People don't fall in love in two weeks."

"Augustus proposed on our first date."

It took Trudy a second to remember that Augustus was Sheila's husband. She pushed away the memories of Truman's proposing the first night they'd slept together.

"You can't publish this," Sheila continued. "You need to talk to Truman first. You owe him that."

"Why?" Trudy was completely taken aback. "Because you swore you wouldn't give him the money if I found out?" At this moment, Trudy hoped the whole world found out. She'd like nothing more than to jerk Truman's share of the money right out from under him. It was what he deserved.

"Just come inside and let me call Truman," urged Sheila.

But Trudy barely heard. "I think I've taken up enough of your valuable time," she managed, and then she turned as regally as she could, and because her knees felt weak, concentrated hard on the stone steps from the porch to the street. As she moved, she reached into her shoulder bag and turned on the cell phone again. "Proposing the first night we slept together?" she suddenly whispered, her heart wrenching. For fifteen million dollars anybody would lie, wouldn't they? Look at the fortune that had been at stake!

When she reached the sidewalk, she stopped in her tracks and groaned.

The cab was nowhere in sight.

11

CAPOTE OPENED TRUMAN'S office door. "Mind if I come in?"

Truman wedged the cell phone under his chin, listening to it ring as Candy twisted in her chair to get a better look at Capote. The uniformed officer was of medium height and build, with short, bristly black hair.

"Looks like you're already in," Truman returned, wondering why Trudy wasn't answering his call. Was Candy right? Had something happened to her? He flashed on some events of the week—a holdup on Fourth Avenue, a cab pileup on the corner of Seventh and West Third. Something must have happened. She wouldn't let anything get in the way of breaking this story. Why wasn't she answering the phone? "Maybe another more important story broke," he murmured. That might explain it.

Or there's no problem at all. Maybe she just didn't want distractions until the story was turned in. He hoped so. This was her moment—*their* moment. His heart squeezed. It wasn't every day a guy found the woman with whom he was supposed to spend the rest of his life.

As he turned off the phone, Capote said, "I dropped by to congratulate you on cracking the Glass Slipper case. Coombs told me all about it."

Usually Truman wouldn't rise to the bait, but this

was Trudy's story. "And you're keeping a lid on it until I take this woman's statement?"

"Sure. The only guy I called was the one I usually talk to over at the *News.*" Capote had said it innocently, but he knew the score. All the officers did. When cases were solved, officers offered tips to the media, a favor they expected to have returned someday. "You know, that guy, Scott Smith-Sanker?"

If he thought it would help Trudy, he'd lunge across the desk at Capote, but as it was, Truman stayed put. He wished Capote had called anybody but Scott, though. This wouldn't be the first time Scott published a story that was rightfully Trudy's. "This is Trudy's story," he repeated.

"That's how it seemed to me," Candy said, even more concerned now, since she'd realized the story was going to embarrass the women who'd had their shoes stolen, and they probably wouldn't press charges. "I don't want somebody else writing it."

"She was definitely sympathetic to you," Truman agreed.

"Well, go find her," said Candy.

Just as Truman rose, pocketing the cell phone, it rang. Relief flooded him. "Trudy?" he said quickly. "Where have you been? Coombs just talked to Capote, and Capote called Scott—"

"It's Ma, Truman."

"What?" He gasped. "Sorry, but I can't talk. Trudy—"

"Was just here."

"There?" What was Trudy doing at his mother's?

"I was on my way out," Sheila said. "Somebody called from Police Plaza. Something about your father.

I'm on my way there right now. Anyway, the doorbell rang, and when I answered it, it was Trudy—"

"Ma," said Truman, frustrated and wanting the information faster than his mother was prepared to deliver it. "What did she say?"

She lunged into a choppy account, and finally finished by saying, "She had the letter from the lottery board with her. She was acting like this was just a big story to her. I'm sorry, Truman. "You love her, don't you?"

His heart missed a beat. "She acted like it was just a story?"

"Yes. I suppose that's all it is for her," Sheila continued, but Truman started to frown at the goading tone. "Is that right?"

"Oh, yes," assured Sheila. "You'd better talk to her. I think she's going to publish a story about me winning the lottery, and you know I can't give you and your brothers the money if people find out about our deal..."

Truman's fingers tightened around the phone. "Aren't you getting tired of all your matchmaking?" he said, barely able to bite back his annoyance. "I can tell you're withholding information. C'mon, Ma. Tell me everything."

"I guess you'll have to ask Trudy."

"I don't know where she is!"

"I really liked her, so I'll be sorry if the relationship doesn't work out for you, but if it doesn't, you're simply going to have to find someone other than Trudy..."

"I don't want anybody other than Trudy," Truman managed.

"Then you better find her. She thinks you wanted to marry her just to get your hands on the lottery money."

"What?" Truman exploded.

But his mother signed off. Switching off the phone, he sank into his chair. No wonder Trudy hadn't called. She was probably getting Gracie Dale to corroborate the story about who'd won the lottery. Why had he fallen for a woman who was this ambitious? He shook his head to clear it of confusion. Surely she didn't really believe he was trying to marry her in order to get the lottery win. Images of their lovemaking crowded into his consciousness—holding her in the dark hours, twining together like vines, waking looking into her face. No, she'd never believe he was using her. They were too close for that. She knew better.

But she was definitely ambitious. Silently, he cursed his mother for introducing a niggling doubt: Had Trudy used him to get information for the lottery story? Had Gracie Dale told her more than she'd let on?

"You have to find her," said Candy.

Truman blinked. He'd almost forgotten Candy was there. "I'm on my way."

"Here." Candy stretched an arm downward, fiddled with something near the floor, and just before she plunked it on his desktop, said, "You might need this."

It was one of the glass slippers she was wearing.

THERE WERE NO CABS. Trudy readjusted the I Love New York bag over her wrist, put her hands on her hips, and stared up and down Hudson Street. Extending her right hand, she waved, just in case. Still, no cabs. Keeping her hand in the air, she gritted her teeth, determined not to let go of the tears brimming in her eyes. Just the other day, Sheila had seemed so nice...so kind...so maternal. But now, she was acting as if Trudy had done something to hurt her son.

It was the other way around, though! It was Trudy who'd been wronged. She'd been used, and now she was losing a career-making story. She moaned. Not an hour ago, her father had been so excited. *News is in your blood,* he'd said.

But really, it was Truman Steele who was in her blood, dancing there like a dervish, spinning around until she felt dizzy. She should have known. Just hours after her own mother had laid eyes on her, she'd dressed and left the hospital where Trudy was born. Pain welled inside her. Trudy had tried to go on. When other girls had mothers to talk to about love, she'd counted her blessings. She'd tried to stay grateful for the things she did have—talent, ambition, interests. She hadn't felt sorry for herself, or placed blame...

"So straighten up," she muttered. She was her father's daughter. A tough cookie. A reporter for whom the story always came first.

Seeing a cab, she waved her arm wildly. "Taxi!"

As it swerved to the curb, she swallowed around a lump in her throat.

It was the same damn driver who'd left her at the Steeles'. "You?"

"Guess it's your lucky day."

She'd rather walk than ride with him, but it would take hours, and there weren't any other cabs, so she got in.

"Where to?"

She tried to tell herself that Truman didn't matter.

She was not only breaking the Glass Slipper, but the lottery story also. Even better, she'd tied them both to the Galapagos oil spill and the plight of the homeless. God, she was good. She shook her head. A mother's foiled attempt to get three bachelor sons married off? A threat to give fifteen million dollars to a wildlife charity unless three New York cops found brides? This would make for great copy. It would sell papers.

But it hurt. Oh, dammit, why did it have to hurt this much?

"The *New York News.*" Pushing Truman from her mind, she couldn't help but add, "And step on it."

CURSING SOFTLY, TRUMAN turned on the siren. It didn't help, so he turned it off and continued inching through traffic toward the corner of Fifth and Thirty-eighth. Driving with one hand, he tried Trudy on the cell phone again. It was ringing, but she wasn't answering. Why not? What was going through her mind? Surely she didn't really think he'd used her.

Leaning out the cruiser window, he craned to get a better look at the bumper-to-bumper traffic.

"A movie," he muttered.

Vaguely, he remembered something about a problematic permit issued to this area. One of the big name directors—somebody like Coppola or Scorcese— wanted to film here. Up ahead, bright fluorescent spotlights flashed on, and as he inched closer, Truman could make out cranes for the mounted cameras, a food service truck and on-location trailers, then his eyes scanned the street. Crowds were forming, the people, mostly office workers from Midtown edging close to blue sawhorses, hoping to catch a glimpse of the celebrities as they shot their scene.

"O'Grady," Truman suddenly called to a mountie who was skirting the crowd, expertly guiding the reins, so the horse dodged a fire hydrant and trotted along the sidewalk.

"That you, Steele?" The officer called, waving as he edged between cars, then stared down at Truman.

Truman didn't waste any time. "I need a favor."

"Anything, buddy."

"I need to borrow your horse." Before O'Grady could answer, Truman was out of the car, and taking the reins.

Sliding off the horse's back, O'Grady said, "I hope you know how to ride."

Truman flashed him a quick grin, his mind already mapping the quickest route to the *New York News* office. He was astride the horse and a half block away before Jack O'Grady registered his parting words, "Don't worry. I'll learn."

TRUDY STARED MUTELY at Dimi. "You can't give Scott the story."

"Dimi knows what he's doing," said Scott, vouching for their boss. "You raced in here, claiming to have a story but I got this tip fifteen minutes ago."

He made fifteen minutes sound like hours. *Which it is in the news business*, Trudy thought. Why had she let Truman suck her in? Other women found love. Her brothers got the *Milton Herald*. And now, Scott was getting the story. The worst thing was that she didn't care. It was definitely the wrong time for heartbreak. *Later*, she thought. *Later, when all this is over, you'll be glad you fought for the story.* Vaguely, she imagined long baths, comfort food, maybe a trip to a very faraway foreign country.

"You do this," she forced herself to say, "and I'll walk out the door." Bringing the plastic bag upward, she slammed it onto the conference table, her anger at Truman's betrayal propelling her as she took an action she should have ages ago. "In here, you'll find the pictures you need. And you're not getting them unless I write this story."

Dimi eased back from the table to make more room for his massive girth. "Trudy, according to your contract, anything you collect while pursuing a story for the *New York News* is the legal property of the *New York News.*"

"I hope you understand," she returned, using a rush of fury she suddenly felt toward Truman, "that I'm tired of playing by unfair rules. I'll eat these photographs, before I hand them to you. I'm no longer available to do Scott's legwork for no credit!" She felt so exploited at the moment! So used!

In a patronizing voice, Scott coaxed, "Don't be a sore loser. Dimi will give you a story."

Her eyes pierced her colleague. "Dimi's not *giving* me anything," she informed him. "I've been on this for weeks. In the streets. Shooting photos. Interviewing the women wearing the shoes, and the one who confessed to the police."

Dimi reached into the bag, rifled through the photos and whistled. Stories about the homeless had been told countless times, but Trudy had an eye for the heartbreaking details that would move readers to tears.

"That man's name is Leon," she said, nodding at the

picture in his hand. "I've got a dynamite interview with him."

While Scott had taken stories out from under her with the ease of a well-lubricated machine, Dimi knew he'd let it happen. And all because he hadn't wanted to train those lovely China-blue eyes on crime scenes. Judging from the pictures, Trudy was going to win, whether he helped her or not. Which meant he'd better help her.

Before he could speak, she played her trump card. "I can tell you who won the fifteen million dollar jackpot."

Scott gaped. "Can't you see she's bluffing, Dimi?"

"I can tie it to the Galapagos Islands and the shoes," she continued, her voice steely. "And with what I've got, I can be at another newspaper tomorrow."

"Listen to her!" Scott exclaimed.

"Whatever she's learned," returned Dimi, "she's learned from watching you. Scott, you're off the story. After I'm finished talking with you, you're back on that subway collision. Trudy, get a guy from the darkroom to look at these photos. After I finish reassigning Scott, I'll hear what you've got on the lottery. And Busey."

She turned at the door, wishing the victory was sweeter. It seemed years, not less than an hour ago, when she'd hugged Truman in the precinct garage. This was supposed to be their moment. But it was empty. For the first time, she'd felt so sure that somebody believed in her, truly believed in her. Now she could barely find her voice. "Yes?"

"This better be good," Dimi warned. "It's tomorrow's cover story."

"COME BACK," TRUDY called over her shoulder, staring at the blank computer screen. Oh God, she'd heard of writer's block, but she'd never actually experienced it. This was the biggest story of her life, but her mind was empty, like a sieve. Everything seemed to have drained out. She couldn't type! It was as if she had absolutely nothing to say.

Except that she wanted Truman.

She'd already been interrupted once—by the delivery of the tropical flowers now sitting on her desk. They'd come with a card that read: *The home team's rooting for you. Love, Dad, Ed, Bob, The Wives, and the whole staff of the* Milton Herald. *You've done us proud!*

She'd nearly broken down and cried. But she had to write the story! If she didn't write it, there'd be nothing to be proud of. But Truman's face never left her mind. She kept recalling how looking into his whiskey-colored eyes made her feel high on life, and how the straight, light-brown strands of his hair that shouldn't have been so special felt like silk on her bare skin. He'd loved her so often, holding her against his chest, letting her cry, lavishly tonguing every inch of her...

There was another knock on the door. "I'm busy!" she snapped, steeling herself against the emotions overwhelming her. "Unless that's you, Dimi, coming to find out more about the lottery story. Then you can come in. You're going to love it," she continued, her fingers poised as if they might start moving on the keyboard—until the second she gave up and swivelled to face the door, saying, "The winner's a housewife who lives down in the Village. She's dividing the money between three bachelor sons, but only if they marry."

She gasped when she saw him.

Truman tensed. The lottery *story*. That's what Trudy had said. And Truman's mother was *the winner*. *A housewife*. Not what she should have been: *my future mother-in-law*. Truman's heart missed a beat as he stared at her. "I thought Ma was just trying to get me to track you down, but maybe I was wrong about you."

She merely stared at him with wide, intense eyes.

It didn't help that she looked so...well, *so Trudy*. In old jeans, sneakers, and the hooded sweatshirt, she looked like a fresh-faced college kid, not an up-and-coming New York reporter who'd do anything for a story. Yes, she looked like a real sweetheart, except for those eyes. Aware and penetrating, they remained fixed on his. His mind flashed on their interaction less than an hour ago in the precinct garage. *I knew it*, he'd said. *All along, you've been sleeping with me for information.* She'd responded, *Better than for your money*. Had she known about his money then?

Right now, Trudy looked as if she'd rather be anywhere in the world but here. "Why'd you come here?"

"To warn you that Capote called Scott."

"Thanks, but I figured that out."

He was still thinking of the lottery story. She'd been trying to get Gracie Dale to talk, and Truman had caught her going through his pockets now—not once, but twice. "The lottery *story?*" he repeated with a softness that belied his mood. Stepping inside the office, he shut the door.

Her eyes were steely. "I'm a reporter. And yeah. It's a story."

"After speaking with my mother," he found himself saying, "you know the rules of the game. If you report this, my brothers won't get their money. I don't care about my part. But I don't want you to take a win from my brothers."

"You don't care about yours?"

He shook his head. "No, but my brothers have dreams. Plans for their share."

"And I should care about that?"

"I take that to mean," he returned coolly, "that you'll do anything for that story?" His eyes narrowed. "Including seduction?"

Trudy's lips slackened then she rose to her feet and circled the desk. "*You* have the nerve to accuse *me*? Let me ask you this. Why would a man who's never been involved suddenly sweep somebody like me off her feet?"

"Somebody like you?" He was thinking she was *perfect*.

"Alone," she said. "Vulnerable."

Was that really how she thought of herself? He thought of Sue. "I *have* been involved."

"Once, ten years ago, and never since."

His voice lowered, and he found himself asking, "Is that what I did, Trudy? Sweep you off your feet?"

Ignoring him, she rushed on. "Was it my lack of experience that attracted you, Truman? My naivete? Did you think, since I was a virgin, that I wouldn't be able to tell the difference between a ploy and real love?"

He gaped at her. "What are you *talking* about?"

"The money." Blue eyes flashed. "Obviously."

"The money?" He registered the hurt in her gaze. Raw and debilitating, he could tell the suspicious emotions were ripping her apart, tearing into her soul.

"Or was it my vulnerability?" she continued. "You were so smart. You knew I was the right kind of woman to target. You knew I was lonely. Without sexual experience. And that I'd marry you in under three months."

Staring deeply into her eyes, he became conscious of how close she was, just a foot away. Deep down, she had to know he hadn't tricked her. Had she treated the lottery win as a mere story, simply because she feared he didn't love her? Suddenly he was sure of it. His throat tightened. "Would you?"

She gasped. "Would I *what?*"

"Marry me, Trudy."

She swallowed with difficulty as if something had lodged in her throat. "We'll never know, will we?"

"Sure, we will." A slow smile curled his lips. He knew he had to give this his best shot. "What if you were only using me for a story?"

"You don't believe that! I'd be incapable of it!"

Now he could see she was blinking back tears, so he moved closer, circling an arm around her back and drawing her against him. Relief washed over him when, despite her anger, she came to him. "You belong here," he murmured, pressing the words into her hair as their hips locked, thighs met, and chests brushed. "Right next to me. I love you, Tru."

She was still tense in his arms. "Why would I believe that?"

He took a deep breath, cursing himself for being ten kinds of fool. "Because I'm going to give my share of the money to the turtles."

She looked thoroughly confused, and her voice was shaky. "Turtles?"

He nodded. "Yeah. The marine iguanas. Penguins. Flightless cormorants. Whatever. We won't keep a dime. All of my share goes to the research foundation on the Galapagos Islands.''

Tears dried in her eyes, she was so utterly astonished. She stared at him as if she'd never seen him before. A paradigm shift, indeed. "You'd actually do that, Tru?"

He nodded. "Consider it done."

She studied him a long, solemn moment. "And I'll only write the Glass Slipper story today," she vowed. "When Dimi comes in, to find out who won the lottery, I'll tell him my sources aren't as good as I thought. I won't tie together the threads...the Galapagos Islands, the lottery, the shoes." She sighed wistfully over the magnitude of the story she was losing. "That will give your brothers time to meet the deadline." She smiled. "After that, of course, the story's mine."

He chuckled softly. "You'd actually do that for me?"

She nodded. "Consider it done."

"But these are moot points unless you marry me. According to Ma, all three of us have to find brides." He held his breath. "As for me, it's you or nobody, Tru."

She exhaled shakily. "Would you have had the same feelings for me if the lottery money wasn't involved?"

"No," he said honestly. "If it hadn't been for the money, I wouldn't have been looking for you, Tru. It was Ma's offer that opened my eyes. And because my eyes were open, I saw you."

"I saw you, too," she whispered. And then, "Of course I'll marry you."

"You're going to cry," he murmured. "That," he added, "or the longer our bodies stayed locked together like this, the more glazed your eyes start to look." He released a throaty hum. "Yes," he murmured. "You've got eyes like smoke. I'm beginning to suspect you're feeling a little lust for your future husband."

"You have a suspicious mind." Wreathing her arms around his neck, she lifted her lips for a kiss that sent a joint shiver through them.

"What can I say?" he returned huskily. "I'm a cop."

She was melting in his arms, her voice hitching with excitement. "Well, we've made the deal. Should we shake on it?"

"You're not getting off that easy," he assured.

"Anything more will have to wait," she murmured wistfully, glancing toward the flowers and blank computer monitor. "It seems you've just single-handedly cured my first-ever case of writer's block."

"And that means I have to wait?"

"Just until tonight."

"It'll be well worth it. Besides," he added, sweeping his mouth to hers once more, his heart swelling, "starting today, we have forever."

She was smiling at him, eyes shining. "Do we, Tru?"

He nodded. "Without even knowing it, I've been waiting for you to walk into my world, Trudy Busey. But until now, I've never known what you'd look like. Or what you'd do for a living. Or where you'd live. All I knew, was that you'd be wearing one of these."

A second later, laughter bubbled from the lips he was about to kiss again—because Truman reached into his back pocket, pulled out a glass slipper and slipped it onto the foot of the woman he loved. "Never walk away from me, Trudy," he murmured.

"I won't," she assured.

And Trudy never did.

* * * * *

...And there's more
BIG APPLE BACHELORS
headed your way!
Here's a sneak preview of
THE SEDUCER,
the second book in Jule McBride's
exciting new miniseries
coming June 2002!

the car, was getting restless. "You mean I'm not the

1

As Sheila Steele opened the front door of the family's New York brownstone, a summer breeze blew inside, dislodging loose gray stands from her pinned back hair. Anxiously smoothing them, she peered out, her heart clutching. Had the caller come because her husband, Augustus, was missing?

When she saw the man on the stoop, her heart sank. A lost tourist, no doubt. He was wearing khaki shorts and a Hawaiian print shirt, and he had shaggy blond hair. Dark blue, almost violet eyes stared from behind black-framed glasses, and a camera was slung around his neck. "Can I help you?"

"Ma?" The man squinted. "It's me, Rex."

Her lips parted in surprise. "I can't believe I didn't even recognize my own son!"

"I came as soon as Sully called with the news about Pop."

Sheila pressed a hand to her heart as Rex stepped into the foyer, giving her a hug and kissing her cheek. "Don't feel bad, Ma. Nobody ever recognizes me. That's the point." Rex had worked undercover for years.

Despite the circumstances of the meeting, Sheila leaned back to study the son who most shared her passions and temperament. "Hard to believe the good-looking man I gave birth to is really under there somewhere."

"He is," Rex assured. Without the wig, contact lenses and cheek pads, he had dark unruly hair and magical hazel eyes that hovered between brown, blue and green. His cheeks were shallow to the point of gaunt, his lips full and sensuous. "My big case finally broke yesterday," he said, "so I spent this morning riding the subway." The Mr. Nice Guy outfit was designed to make him a target for transit pickpockets.

Sheila offered a watery smile. In other circumstances, she would have laughed. "How many times have you been robbed this morning?"

"Three," Rex admitted. "So far. I arrested them all."

She took a deep breath. "Well, c'mon inside. Everybody's in the courtyard."

He followed her down a long hallway. "Everybody?"

"Both your brothers. Sullivan got here first. And Truman brought the woman he's been dating, Trudy Busey."

"The one I met the other day at lunch? From the *New York News?*"

Sheila nodded. "They were at the newspaper when I called Truman." Sheila grasped Rex's hand for support. "I'm glad you're here, Rexie."

Since his mother hadn't called him that for years, Rex's heart wrenched. "Pop's gonna be fine," he assured, his voice soft, his eyes focused on the summery light at the end of the hallway; through a screen door, riotous leaves sprawled in the courtyard garden that was one of his mother's many passions.

When they reached the door, she turned to face him. "I really can't imagine what's happened to your father." She sighed. "You were supposed to go on vacation tomorrow?"

"To Storm Island. Just off Long Island. I told you."

"That's where the boat was anchored before it..."

Exploded. Rex didn't blame her for not wanting to voice the word. "Pop knew I was going there."

"Maybe he intended to meet you," she probed, her voice catching. "Maybe that's why he was there, Rex. Did he say anything to you about whatever he's involved in?"

Rex shook his head. "Nothing. If Pop wanted help," Rex murmured, wishing it didn't hurt so much to admit it, "he'd have gone to Truman or Sully. You know that, Ma." In the deepening warmth of her gaze, Rex could feel her quiet understanding, and he rested a thumb on her chin, promising, "I'll do whatever I can. This is Pop we're talking about. Starting tomorrow, I've got a month off."

"But your vacation..."

"Doesn't matter." More than anyone, she knew Rex lived for vacations, when he fled to the sands of unknown beaches, often registering in hotels under an assumed name so no one but his parents could find him. For one month a year, he pursued interests unlike those of his father, brothers and most Manhattan law enforcement officers—reading, writing, painting and cooking. "C'mon," he murmured. "Let's see what Sully's found out."

It wasn't good, Rex realized, after seating his mother and himself at a round table, shaded by a leafy oak. He glanced at Truman who'd come in his uniform, then at their oldest brother, Sullivan, who was captain of the precinct nearest the house. He was wearing a suit and leaning against the oak tree. Both brothers, with their light brown hair and whiskey eyes, were the spitting image of Augustus. Rex looked like their mother.

"Dimi's refusing to run the article I've been writing about the NYPD, using your family as a prototype," Trudy was saying, her blue eyes snapping with righteous indignation. "It was supposed to be in tomorrow's *News*, but Dimi won't publish anything about you until he's sure Mr. Steele's done nothing wrong." She groaned, frustrated. "I can't believe this! Now, more than ever, your names should be in the paper! We need to figure out what's happened!"

Rex squinted at his brother's girlfriend. Judging from the light that came into her eyes when she glanced at Truman, she'd completely fallen for him, and Rex felt happy for his little brother. Rex figured Dimi was Trudy's boss. "What exactly was the article about?"

"For the past two weeks, Trudy's been on a ride-along in the patrol car with me," Truman explained, rising from her side. He started pacing, the hands on his hips slipping down to a billy club and holstered gun. "The article was supposed to be good PR for the city. You know, a day in the life of a cop. It was going to press tonight."

"Now I remember you mentioning it," said Rex.

"I was at my desk writing it," Trudy added, "as well as another story when Sheila called." Pausing, she swallowed hard, her eyes darting to Sheila's. "I'm sorry I was so angry when I came over earlier today..."

Rex was less concerned with whatever previously transpired between the women than with collecting facts pertaining to Augustus's disappearance. "You say they're pulling the story, little brother?"

Truman nodded, stepping behind Trudy, placing his hands on her shoulders and massaging them. "The rumor is that Pop's on the take."

"That's ridiculous!" Sheila exclaimed with a sharp intake of breath. "Earlier, when Trudy came over, I'd just gotten a call from Police Plaza. They didn't even do me the courtesy of coming by the house to tell me he disappeared! And he's been on the force thirty-three years! He's never taken a dime, except from his paycheck, but they made me go all the way downtown to tell me he's..."

Rex's fingers closed tightly over hers. "It's going to be okay, Ma."

Looking unconvinced, Sully thrust both hands deep into his trouser pockets, further relaxing against the oak. Red lines on the bark marked their heights as kids, but Sully, now thirty-six, towered over all the marks. "That internal affairs woman who's been on my back is heading up the investigation."

Rex cursed under his breath. "Judith Hunt?"

"Yeah," returned Sully. "According to her, the money in the city's Citizens' Contribution Fund is missing. She took a crew to Storm Island to dive for whatever's left of the boat."

"Do they really think your father could steal public money?" whispered Sheila. "After all his years of loyalty and service?"

Sully sighed, his eyes lighting briefly on his brothers. "I hate to have to say this, but they've got Pop withdrawing money at the bank. On videotape."

Sheila was dumbfounded. "Your father withdrew money?"

Sully paused, then said, "Over ten million."

Sheila was reeling. "Dollars? Of public money? And a bank let him take it? There's got to be a mistake! He'd never..."

"He wire-transferred the money from Citicorp,"

countered Sully, "then picked it up elsewhere in two suitcases."

Sheila stared. "In suitcases? That's impossible. You know your father. He'd never do anything wrong."

"The videotape's incriminating," returned Sully simply.

Stricken, she whispered, "What if he's dead?"

Rex's fingers fell between hers. "C'mon now," he chided gently. "Pop's too tough to die."

"You've got a point there, Rex," agreed Truman.

"We'll figure this whole thing out," Sully assured.

"I just don't get it," interjected Trudy, lifting her hands to twine them with Truman's. "He's been working at Police Plaza, so he's completely out of the line of fire. The only logical explanation is that he stumbled onto something..."

Rex raised an eyebrow. "Such as?"

Trudy shrugged. "Maybe somebody was tampering with the Citizens' Contribution Fund, and he's stowing the money somewhere until he can prove whatever he found."

Rex rifled a hand through the wig he wore, wishing it didn't itch in the summer heat. "Even if Pop discovered someone mishandling funds, taking a fortune from a city account is a strange way of fixing the problem. He had to know he'd be seen on tape. Why wasn't the money invested, anyway? Isn't that the responsibility of the Dispersion Committee?"

Sullivan shrugged. "All good questions, Rex. But the fact is, we haven't got a clue as to what's happened. Not yet. all anybody knows for sure is that the boat usually docks at the Manhattan Yacht Club and Pop was on deck when it left the slip."

Rex visualized the mile of sidewalk fronting Battery

Park City, overlooking the Hudson River and Statue of Liberty. "That's a pricey place to dock. Donald Trump and Henry Kravis keep boats there. Who owned it?"

"Registered under a false name," supplied Sullivan. "I'm still looking."

Rex shook his head. "We need to find that out."

"And if your father's still alive," added Sheila shakily.

"No bodies have been recovered," Rex reminded gently. When everyone fell silent, he cast brooding eyes into the garden, long enough that his gaze unfocused, making the world appear to be a blur of color. Mentally, Rex cursed his father. Why didn't he bother to notice how often his wife's face was drawn with worry? She strived so hard to make their lives wonderful. And now this. Unlike his brothers, it was Rex who remembered his mother's worry when Augustus didn't make it home from stakeouts. And the excruciating times—sometimes minutes, sometimes hours—between hearing a cop was killed in the line of duty, then being told the victim wasn't Augustus. No doubt, things were as Trudy said. Augustus had discovered wrongdoing, then set out in high macho style to catch the culprit himself.

Which meant Rex would have to find him. *A far cry from the last time Ma called us here,* Rex thought ruefully. Only a few weeks ago, she'd received one of the biggest lottery wins in New York City history, and driven by a good heart and desperate desire to see her sons happily married, she'd made an unthinkable deal: If Sullivan, Rex and Truman kept silent about the money and married within three months, she'd divide fifteen million dollars between them. Otherwise, she'd give the money to a wildlife research station on the Galapagos Islands.

Rex had meant what he'd said that day. As far as he was concerned, the Galapagos Islands could have the money. Rex had spent more than one summer vacation lounging on the rocky beaches, sketching the animals.

"We can't find soul mates in three months," he'd argued that day, amused and intrigued by their mother's inventive way of encouraging them to find spouses.

"She said *wives*, not *soul mates*," Truman had argued.

But for Rex, they were the same. Besides, to him marriage was just a piece of paper. Maybe because he was a lawman, he wanted something that transcended legalities. He wanted mystery. Romance. Poetry. Soul-searing sex. A lover whose warm body would twine with his, melting his heart. Each year, on his annual sojourn, he imagined he might find her. He'd always envisioned meeting her while wandering on a deserted beach, or in the dunes, and making love to her in the hot sand while sea foam washed over their bare bodies.

Not that it mattered now Augustus was missing, which meant Rex would be looking for *him* on Storm Island—not a woman.

Rex said a silent goodbye to the month-long hiatus he got only once a year. At least he'd already forwarded his mail to Casa Eldora, the two-bedroom cottage he'd rented on Storm Island under the name Ned Lloyd. In the brochure, the waterfront place looked perfect. A sexy-voiced realtor whose laughter sounded like crystal bells had introduced herself as Pansy Hanley and said she'd look forward to meeting him.

Since the call, Rex hadn't been able to get her voice out of his mind. When they met, he'd planned to do what he always did on vacations: drop the mask. Lose the disguises. Trade in his sidearm for a fishing rod, and deli sandwiches for fresh-caught fish. He'd already imagined himself asking Pansy Hanley to Casa Eldora for dinner...maybe more. Now he squeezed his mother's hand. "If Pop's out there, I'll find him, Ma. Don't worry."

So much for this year's hopes of meeting a dream lover.

* * * * *

Or at least that's what Rex Steele thinks!
But Storm Island offers more than danger.
It offers pleasures beyond anything
he's ever imagined....

COOPER'S  CORNER

In April 2002 you are invited to three wonderful weddings in a very special town...

A Wedding at Cooper's Corner

USA Today bestselling author

Kristine Rolofson
Muriel Jensen
Bobby Hutchinson

Ailing Warren Cooper has asked private investigator David Solomon to deliver three precious envelopes to each of his grandchildren. Inside each is something that will bring surprise, betrayal...and unexpected romance!

And look for the exciting launch of *Cooper's Corner*, a NEW 12-book continuity from Harlequin— launching in August 2002.

HARLEQUIN®
Makes any time special ®

Visit us at www.eHarlequin.com

PHWCC

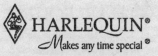

If you enjoyed what you just read,
then we've got an offer you can't resist!

Take 2 bestselling
love stories FREE!
Plus get a FREE surprise gift!

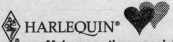
HINT7CH

HARLEQUIN Temptation

It's hot...and it's out of control!

This spring, the forecast is hot and steamy!
Don't miss these bold, provocative, ultra-sexy books!

PRIVATE INVESTIGATIONS by Tori Carrington
April 2002

Secretary-turned-P.I. Ripley Logan never thought her first job
would have her running for her life—or crawling into
a stranger's bed....

ONE HOT NUMBER by Sandy Steen
May 2002

Accountant Samantha Collins may be good with numbers, but
she needs some work with men...until she meets sexy but
broke rancher Ryder Wells. Then she decides to make him a
deal—her brains for his bed. Sam's getting the better of the
deal, but hey, who's counting?

WHAT'S YOUR PLEASURE? by Julie Elizabeth Leto
June 2002

Mystery writer Devon Michaels is in a bind. Her publisher has
promised her a lucrative contract, *if* she makes the jump to
erotic thrillers. The problem: Devon can't write a love scene to
save her life. Luckily for her, Detective Jake Tanner is an
expert at "hands-on" training....

Don't miss this thrilling threesome!

HARLEQUIN®
Makes any time special ®

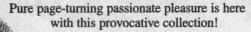